"My father has nothing to do with this! Why would you even think that?"

"One of the guys out there," TJ answered simply. "He remembered that you were dating Ricky and your father didn't like him. Made some threats against him, in fact."

"That is absolutely not what happened. I don't know how long you've been here in Melfield, Detective Douglas, but you should talk to some of the people who knew my father. He was a good man. He got along with everyone and would never hurt anybody. Ever! I refuse to sit here and let you ruin his legacy by starting rumors about him."

"I'm not starting any rumors, Miss Fenton, I'm just telling you what I heard. Obviously, the rumors have already been here. If that body beside the church does turn out to be your old boyfriend, it's likely those guys on the excavation crew won't be the only ones with rumors to spread. If there's anything you'd like to tell me about what happened back then, I suggest you do so...before the rumors really do start flying."

Not the typical pastor's wife, **Susan Gee Heino** has been writing romance since the first day her husband bought her a computer, hoping she would help him with church bulletins. Instead, she started writing. A lifelong follower of Christ, Susan has two children in college and lives in rural Ohio. She spends her days herding cats and feeding chickens, crafting stories with hope, humor and happily-ever-afters. She invites you to sign up for her newsletter at susangh.com.

GRAVE SECRETS

SUSAN GEE HEINO

LOVE INSPIRED
INSPIRATIONAL ROMANCE

LOVE INSPIRED®
INSPIRATIONAL ROMANCE

Recycling programs
for this product may
not exist in your area.

ISBN-13: 978-1-335-63344-6

Grave Secrets

Love Inspired
22 Adelaide St. West, 41st Floor
Toronto, Ontario M5H 4E3, Canada
www.LoveInspired.com

Printed in U.S.A.

And above all these things put on charity, which is the bond of perfectness. And let the peace of God rule in your hearts, to the which also ye are called in one body; and be ye thankful.
—*Colossians* 3:14–15

This book is dedicated to my pastor.
I am very, very blessed to also be able
to call him my husband. Thank you, Jack Heino,
for all the years of laughter and love, for your faith
and devotion, and for buying me that computer
waaaaaay back when we couldn't even afford
a desk to put it on.

Chapter One

The morning sunshine was optimistically bright. Today, however, might bring good news…or very bad news. Carlie Fenton honestly wasn't sure which she was hoping for.

What she *hadn't* been hoping for was a pothole that caused her car to jolt, her arm to jerk and her coffee to spill all over her nice blouse. There wasn't time to turn around and go back to her apartment to change, though. The bank appraiser would be waiting at the site and she was already running late.

Unfortunately, she'd just have to show up with a coffee stain. So much for giving the best impression. In this case, being on time seemed more important than being neat.

Their work today would determine just how much of a loan she would need to buy the old Epiphany Church property and renovate it. It would take a lot of money—probably more than a small-town bank really wanted to loan to a single woman who had just left a perfectly good job in the city. More than once, Carlie had wondered if she was completely off her rocker to even consider such a thing. But then again…she wanted this.

Leaving the quiet village of Melfield behind her, Carlie could see her goal in the distance. Tall and white, Epiphany's steeple rose over rolling farmlands, the church set in an island of towering oaks and cemetery lawn. Even in its derelict state, the old building was a beacon of hope.

And boy, did Carlie need some of that in her life.

Joining them on-site today would be a contractor with heavy equipment for excavating. He was probably waiting there with the appraiser already. Carlie tried not to be anxious about what they would find, but her nerves just wouldn't calm down.

For years, the church had struggled with standing water around the foundation. A leaky cistern, everyone said, causing the foundation to bow and crack. Several attempts had been made to solve the problems over time but nothing had worked, and eventually, the congregation just gave up. Carlie still hadn't quite come to terms with that.

She had loved Epiphany Church all of her life. It had been her father's ministry. He'd spent most of his career serving the little congregation here, just outside Melfield, Kentucky. It still felt like a betrayal that after he'd passed away, the people had simply shuttered the doors and joined up with a newer, larger church in town. It was as if her father's work—his legacy—had meant nothing to them.

But now she was back, and she was determined to rescue this beautiful building. All she needed was money. Unfortunately, the bank felt the cost to repair the building was far beyond its worth. The appraiser insisted the foundation was too badly deteriorated. Before they would even consider a loan, she would have to bring in a contractor—at her expense—and show proof that the foundation could be saved.

So here she was, pulling into the gravel parking area. It was sad to see the place so unkempt. The little cemetery beside the church—and the parsonage just beyond that—was nearly lost behind weeds and overgrown bushes. Greenery of all sorts was bursting out in the June heat. While her parents had lived here, the grass had been well manicured, the plantings trimmed, and profusions of flowers had blossomed everywhere. Today sprawling shrubs and strangled perennials were all that was left of the landscaping.

The bank appraiser's modest sedan was parked in the church lot, along with two pickup trucks bearing the name of the contractor who would be doing the work today. A flatbed trailer sat empty—it had probably been used to haul in the backhoe that would be needed for digging. All this was expected. What surprised her, though, was the other vehicle present.

A sheriff's cruiser.

Parking quickly, she took the last swallow of her coffee and headed around to the back of the church. Tall trees shaded the area. Birds chirped and swooped between the branches and the many peaks and angles of the church roof. She expected to hear the loud rumble of heavy machinery, but instead, the work site was oddly quiet.

Several people stood idle, watching a tall man in a dark suit as he peered into a recently excavated hole. As he studied the soil piled around him, he jotted in his notebook. Carlie didn't recognize him. Based on his intent focus and the set of his jaw, what he saw in the cracked foundation here definitely concerned him. Carlie could feel tension in the air, radiating from everyone.

This could not be good. She looked over at Kim Daley, the appraiser. Had Kim brought in one of the bank executives? But she just gave Carlie a wide-eyed, questioning look. Before Carlie could ask what was going on, the man in the suit glanced up and noticed her.

"You must be Miss Fenton," he said, checking something in his notebook.

His eyes were a surprising green; even from fifteen feet away, Carlie couldn't help but notice them. What she didn't notice was a polite smile of greeting—because it wasn't there. Everything about the man was deadly serious.

"Yes, I'm Carlie Fenton," she replied, stepping forward. Nervous energy danced inside her.

The man nodded. "I'm told your father was the minister of this church?"

"He was," she replied, not sure why he needed this information. "He passed away five years ago."

"How long was he minister here?"

"He served at Epiphany more than twenty-five years."

"I see," the man said, making another note. "So he would have overseen the last work that was done on this area of the building."

"Well, he acted with the church board on things like that. I don't remember who they hired to do the actual work. I'm sure it's all in the old church records somewhere, if—"

"Your family lived in that house just over there during that time, correct?"

"Yes, that's the parsonage," she replied, frustrated with all the useless questions. "Look, I know there are significant problems with the building. If you're from the bank, I assure you that the first appraiser made me well aware of them. Whatever issues you're finding down there, I'm very confident we can repair them."

"I'm not from the bank," he said simply. "And there's no repairing what we found down there."

"What have you found?" she asked, moving closer to join him at the edge of the excavation to see for herself. A muddy stone tripped her and she staggered gracelessly. The man caught her before she tumbled into the hole.

He pulled her back, but the brief glimpse she got into the newly dug opening was enough. She gasped for breath.

"Is that a…a *body* down there?"

She used that word because she didn't know what else to say. What she'd seen could hardly be called a *body*. In the hole, she could make out a form—it was muddied, misshapen and mostly reclaimed by the earth, but there was just enough to it that she had no doubt. Someone was buried there. Whoever it was could be little more than a skeleton now, but she recognized tennis shoes and scraps of fabric that had possibly been jeans. The head and shoulders were still covered, but the torso was wrapped in what must have been a jacket at one time. Almost all of it was the same color as the dirt, but one area of the jacket had apparently been folded and protected. It was unfolded now, and she could clearly see the colors: red and white, with embroidery. It was a high school letterman jacket. That image would be seared forever in her mind.

"There *is* a body down there," the man confirmed, helping her right herself at a safe distance. "I'm Lieutenant Detective Douglas from the sheriff's office. Your crew found this earlier today and called it in."

Now she understood why the work had stopped and everyone was just standing around. A quick glance at Mr. Johnson, her contractor, and she could see the stricken look on his face. He nodded, confirming the detective's words.

"We thought we'd get an early start," Mr. Johnson said. "Dillon was on the backhoe. We were watching pretty close, making sure we didn't break into that old cistern everyone told us was around here. Then we... well, then we found *him*."

One of the other guys chimed in. "We know who it is, too. It's that kid who went missing. Ricky Something-or-other."

Carlie's stomach jerked into a knot. "*Ricky LeMaster*?"

"Did you know him?" the detective asked, positioning himself between her and the hole.

She could hardly catch her breath. The vision burned in her mind was a heavy weight, almost crushing her. Could that dirty, twisted form there really be Ricky? It wasn't possible. It couldn't be. But the red-and-white jacket... *Ricky had loved his school jacket.*

"Yeah," she replied softly. "I knew him."

The detective put another mark in his notebook. "I think we need to talk."

Detective TJ Douglas was used to having unwilling conversation partners. Carlie Fenton was definitely that. Whatever she knew about this body buried beside her father's old church was not something she wanted to discuss.

Several of the guys on the work crew seemed eager to talk, though. TJ wasn't ready to entertain all their suspicions and rehashing of local lore. He needed facts, and quite frankly, Miss Fenton seemed to be his best shot at getting them. If he could pull some out of her.

When the call came in about the discovery of possible human remains, TJ had been nearby, looking into vandalism at a farm just up the road. Three other detectives worked under him in the investigative division, but none of them had been positioned to get there as quickly as TJ could. He'd arrived at the old church within minutes of receiving the summons. A couple deputies and one of his detectives had appeared shortly after Miss Fenton.

TJ put Detective Scheuster in charge of the others to secure the scene. They would begin a proper investigation, but in the meantime, he wanted to get some more answers from Miss Fenton. He asked the bank appraiser to open the church building and took Carlie inside where they could talk uninterrupted. She followed him, moving mechanically, giving the impression she was still half in shock.

The air inside was stale; clearly, the place had been closed up for a while. There was a layer of dust over everything, but not enough to block out the sunlight that filtered in over the arched window above the front door. A barren entryway greeted them, offering no welcome besides a few yellowed bulletins pinned to a corkboard on the wall. One dusty raincoat hung on the long coatrack.

Ahead, the doors to the sanctuary were propped open. Huge stained glass windows brought multicolored light into the spacious area, creating an almost ethereal feel. TJ led her in and watched as she took in the sight and the feel of the place. She must have grown up here, must know every inch of the building and its surroundings. Just how much did she know about that body outside?

Rows of well-worn pews faced expectantly forward, as if just waiting for the congregation to return. The walls had empty areas where festive banners or seasonal trimmings had probably once hung. An ornately carved cross still rose over the altar, reminding TJ that they were in a sacred place.

He scanned his notebook, but really he was studying Miss Fenton. She was dressed professionally—tailored but loose black slacks and a crisp white blouse. A slight coffee stain indicated she had hurried this morning. He found that little flaw disarming.

The rest of her was perfectly put together. Her ash-blond hair was combed into a neat ponytail, with the humidity of the day bringing out a hint of curls around the nape of her neck. She wore little makeup, if any, and her earrings were delicate drop pearls. Despite nervousness, she moved gracefully as they entered the sanctuary.

She paused in the aisle, clutching the leather strap of her handbag. He could hear her take short, choppy breaths. From the corner of his eye, he could see that her focus settled on the empty pulpit at the front. When TJ invited her to sit in one of the pews, she jumped.

"I'm sorry," he said. "Is it difficult for you to be here?"

"I haven't been back since…well, for quite a while."

"I understand," he said, mostly out of habit. It was important to create a sense of comfort and rapport with people. The more at ease they felt, the more they would share with him.

He waited, knowing that silence was often the best encouragement to get people to talk.

Finally, she spoke. "After my father's funeral, this place didn't quite seem like home anymore, you know?"

"I can imagine," he said patiently. "You were living here at the time?"

"No, I was just finishing up law school."

"Law school?"

"At University of Kentucky. I offered to put that on hold, to come back and help my mom, but she wouldn't hear of it."

"I take it your father's death was unexpected?"

"Massive heart attack on a Sunday afternoon," she replied, her voice dropping low. "Yeah. That was unexpected."

"I'm very sorry."

"Thanks. I've never been very good with surprises. Like that body out there… That was seriously unexpected, too."

"Was it?"

He realized his mistake even as he spoke the words. He should have been more careful with his phrasing, even though the question needed to be asked. Her eyes grew fierce and her voice was short and clipped.

"Of course it was! What sort of question is that? You think I *knew* someone was buried there?"

Her emotions were stretched thin right now, obviously. Finding a body next to the church where she grew up would be traumatizing for anyone. Still, the more emotional her response, the more honest it would be. She didn't have time to put up any defenses—that was the way he wanted it. If she knew anything, or ever suspected anything, about how that body got there, she might give it away now, without realizing.

She'd probably hate his questions and hate him for asking them. But he wasn't there to make friends. Carlie Fenton might resent him, but he couldn't worry about that. He'd run the risk of alienating her in the hopes that he might get the most honest, instinctive answers.

"I don't have enough information to think anything yet, Miss Fenton," he replied, measuring his tone. "But why did those men out there immediately assume it might be your friend Ricky?"

"I don't know. We don't have a lot of missing persons here in Melfield. I guess when they dug up a body, Ricky is the first person they thought of."

"And you," he continued. "Is he the first person *you* thought of, too?"

"I didn't think of anyone," she shot back. "I looked down there in that hole and… I saw what looked like a body. I had no idea who it was."

"Then someone suggested Ricky. Did that seem reasonable to you?"

"Maybe. I don't know! How can we tell they didn't accidentally dig into one of the plots from the cemetery? Maybe things shifted over time, or maybe someone didn't keep careful records and there were burials closer to the building than we knew."

"Of course we'll look into that," he assured her. "But

you didn't deny the possibility that it could be your friend. When did Ricky disappear?"

"About a dozen years ago, when we were in high school. I was still a sophomore, but Ricky was a senior."

"And he just went missing?"

"He ran away right before graduation. No one knew why. He just left."

"He ran away?"

"Yes… At least, that's what everyone thought, although…"

"Although what?"

"It just didn't make sense. Why would he leave before graduation? He had everything to look forward to. Why not wait a month, get his diploma, then take off, if he was so eager to leave?"

"Maybe he was in some kind of trouble. Do you know anything about that?"

She shrugged, chewing her lip as she considered her answer. "You mean trouble with the police?"

"Maybe not the police, but with anyone else… With your father, for instance?"

Now he might have gone too far. She looked ready to end the conversation and storm off.

"My father has nothing to do with this! Why would you even think that?"

"One of the guys out there," he answered simply. "He remembered that you were dating Ricky and your father didn't like him. Made some threats against him, in fact."

"That is absolutely *not* what happened. I don't know how long you've been here in Melfield, Detective Douglas, but you should talk to some of the people who knew my father. He was a good man. He got along with ev-

eryone and would never hurt anybody. Ever! I refuse
to sit here and let you ruin his legacy by starting rumors about him."

"I'm not starting any rumors, Miss Fenton, I'm just
telling you what I heard. Obviously, the rumors have
already been here. If that body beside the church *does*
turn out to be your old boyfriend, it's likely those guys
on the excavation crew won't be the only ones with rumors to spread. If there's anything you'd like to tell me
about what happened back then, I suggest you do so...
before the rumors really do start flying."

Chapter Two

The last thing Carlie wanted to do was travel back in time and relive those months twelve years ago. It was a difficult time for her, for her family and for the whole community. She'd thought she'd gotten over it long ago, but after today's discovery...maybe not.

"Fine, I'll tell you what I know," she said, taking a deep breath before launching into the full explanation. "I dated Ricky LeMaster twelve years ago. It wasn't anything serious, and there was no sordid feud with my father or anything like that. Ricky and I had a couple classes together in school and we went out."

"You both went to high school here in Melfield?"

"Yes, Melfield High."

"I take it your school colors are red and white?"

"They are," she replied. "And before you ask, I'll admit that did look like one of our high school letter jackets on...the body."

"I see." He jotted this down in his notebook. "How long did you know him?"

"Just a year or so. He transferred from another

school. But we had some friends in common, and he started coming to church here, so we hung out. He was a senior, and I was flattered, I guess, that he noticed me. It didn't take long, though, before I knew it wasn't going to work."

"Why is that?" the detective asked, turning back to his notes.

She was glad for the notebook. It was much easier to talk to the man when he wasn't looking at her with those striking green eyes. His chiseled features and tailored suit made him stand out from the rest of the rural population here. He would have looked even more out of place if not for his unruly dark hair.

"We just didn't have much in common, that's all," she responded. "I was into academics, the church youth group, French club… He was kind of a jock, and he really liked to party."

"You mean, drinking and drugs, that sort of thing?"

"Not drugs, but he and his buddies drank a lot of beer," she clarified. "On the weekends after ball games, they'd go out to a field and drink beer, then drive around in someone's car, throwing cans out the windows and yelling at cows. Just the usual teenage stuff here in the country. But I wasn't interested in that."

"You were the preacher's kid, after all. No wonder your father didn't like this boy."

"Oh, my father didn't know about any of that! He thought Ricky was just fine, at first."

"But then…?"

"Then I broke up with him. Ricky didn't take it very well."

He nodded and made more notes. "Tell me about that."

"Like I said, it was never serious between us. Still, he was pretty upset when I broke it off."

"What did he do?"

She took a deep breath. All of this seemed like another lifetime ago. Really, it was. She hadn't thought about Ricky in ages. She was embarrassed to realize the complete lack of concern she'd had for him after he was gone. And now, considering that maybe he hadn't run away but had met a much more horrible fate…she regretted some of the anger she'd felt toward him.

"He wasn't a bad kid," she said finally. "Mostly he was annoying. He called and texted too much and stopped by the house at odd hours. When he was drinking, though…that's when things got kind of scary."

"He threatened you?"

"Yeah. I didn't take it seriously at first, but it was hard to ignore. He started spreading rumors about me at school, ranting on social media, too. I really didn't like that."

"I can imagine. How did your parents react?"

How *did* they react? She had to pause for a moment to think back. She wished they hadn't needed to react at all.

Growing up as the only child of a well-loved minister meant she had learned from an early age that all eyes were upon her. It was like living in a fishbowl—everyone knew what their family had for dinner, when her mother hung laundry on the clothesline, if Carlie was struggling in school. She had learned never to do anything that would draw the wrong kind of attention or reflect poorly on her parents. An ugly breakup with a rowdy boyfriend was the last thing she'd wanted to be involved in.

"At first, they told me to turn the other cheek, so to speak," she replied. "But then things started happening here at the church. Pots of flowers were smashed, the flag on the flagpole got stolen, the big church sign had toilet paper on it. Then our mailbox at the parsonage was bashed in, and someone broke the lock on the cemetery shed."

"You hadn't experienced any of this before?"

"No, and it seemed too coincidental that it would happen just when I was going through all that with Ricky."

"So your father confronted him?"

"He did, but only after we'd been putting up with threats and harassment for a couple months. It wears you down, you know?"

He nodded but kept peppering her with questions. "What happened between them?"

She hated talking about this, but he needed to know. As he'd mentioned, people loved to gossip, and rumors were inevitable. She would far rather have him get the truth from her than to start listening to some of the crazy things people might say.

"Ricky showed up at church one Sunday morning… My father would never turn anyone away. I tried to avoid him, but after service was over, Ricky followed me out to the parking lot and started hounding me."

"In what way?"

"He kept stepping in front of me, wouldn't let me get back into the building or go home to the parsonage. He was taunting me, bragging that he had other girlfriends, that I was boring and stuck-up... Stuff like that."

"So your father threatened him?"

"No!"

"He didn't? From what I've heard—"

"Who have you been talking to? Where are you getting your information already?"

"Before you arrived, Miss Fenton. Like I said, the guys on-site immediately started talking. I can only go on what they said."

"None of those guys know anything! They weren't there that day. I'm telling you what really happened between my father and Ricky. You can go on that, Detective."

She knew her voice was rising but she couldn't help it. This man's constant barrage, his unflagging calm, his cold detachment as he blatantly hinted that her father might have done something horribly wrong really irked her. To sit here with a stranger, in this place that used to be so special to her, and have to defend her father against such awful insinuations poured salt on every wound she'd ever had. And she'd had plenty. This wasn't the first time people had whispered about them. These weren't the first rumors about her father's interactions with Ricky.

They were the worst, however. She'd never heard them repeated by a detective until today. Then again, no one had ever found a body in the churchyard before.

Detective Douglas persisted. "So your father didn't make any threats?"

"No! I mean...not really. My father saw how Ricky

was pestering me…and he suspected he'd been the one doing all that other stuff, too, so he was upset."

"He was angry?"

"Of course he was angry! Anyone would have been. He came storming out, he raised his voice, he told Ricky to leave and never bother me again. He said…"

"Go on, Miss Fenton. What did your father tell the boy?"

"He warned Ricky to stop harassing me."

"The word I heard was *threatened*. Did he threaten the boy?"

"Look, my father was a good man…a peaceful man. He would never hurt anyone!"

"But did he *threaten* anyone?"

"He simply told Ricky to quit causing trouble for us. He said if he didn't stop, well…he said he would make him stop. For good."

She hated the way that sounded. The detective's expression gave away nothing about what he thought, but she knew. There was no way around it—her own words had practically confirmed whatever rumor the man must have heard.

"That pretty much sounds like a threat," Detective Douglas said simply.

"But he didn't mean he would hurt Ricky!" Carlie insisted. "Look, Detective—"

"Call me TJ."

"Detective Douglas," she said, with special emphasis so he would understand that she was not about to let him charm her. If he thought his perfect smile and peridot eyes would lure her into confirming whatever stupid notion he had of her father being some kind of monster, he would be disappointed.

"Yes, Miss Fenton?"

"My father meant that he would inform Ricky's parents or call the authorities, that's all. He just wanted Ricky to stop bothering me, stop damaging church property!"

"And did it stop after that?"

"Yes, it did."

"And that was just about the time Ricky disappeared?"

She had to think about that. It was so long ago. She honestly hadn't pondered any of this for years. "I really don't know for sure. I just remember that day, and then...it wasn't very long before he was gone."

"The next day? Next week? Another month?"

"I don't know!"

"Your father got angry, made threats, and then Ricky just disappeared. You never wondered about that, Miss Fenton?"

"I told you—Ricky left town. He was eighteen, he liked to party, he was kind of rebellious. No one ever suggested anything other than he just ran away."

"He took off one day, out of the blue."

"Yes. It was big news around here. His family looked everywhere, the police were involved, people put up posters, and it was in the newspaper for a year. I felt just awful about it. My dad did, too."

"I would expect your father might be glad to have him gone. Just why did he feel so awful about it?"

"Because my father was a decent man who cared about people," she snapped.

The detective's meaning had been obvious. He just would not let go of the idea that Carlie's father was somehow involved in Ricky's disappearance. How dare he sit here in this place of worship and make such cruel accusations.

"I think we are done with questions here, Detective," she said sharply. "We don't even know for sure if that *is* Ricky LeMaster out there. Shouldn't you be investigating that first, before you convict my father of some murder that—I promise you—he did not commit?"

Detective Douglas flicked his notebook shut and turned his focus back on her. To her surprise, he smiled. Suddenly, here was that warm greeting he'd denied her earlier. Oh, but the man knew how to manipulate.

"You're right," he said calmly. "A positive ID will have to be made. I really appreciate your time today. If it turns out this body is not your friend Ricky LeMaster, then perhaps he's still out there somewhere giving other young women a hard time."

He was trying to be charming, but she refused to fall for it. "I would rather think he's grown up a bit since then…wherever he is."

"It would be nice to think he's grown up at all," he added. "But whether we find this is Ricky or not, someone wearing a high school letter jacket is buried beside your father's church, Miss Fenton. You will be available if I have any more questions, won't you?"

"Yes, I'll be available. I'm as eager to solve this as you are, Detective."

"Good. Oh, one more thing. I know you've only recently moved back here to Melfield. I would hate for you to plan on leaving town again soon."

"You know you have no right to keep me here, don't you?"

"I would never dream of infringing on your rights, Miss Fenton. I know a few things about the law, too. You're free to go, of course."

"Yes, I am. Now I wish you well with your investigation. If you need me, I'll help any way I can. I don't have anything to hide."

"I'm glad to hear that," he said. "I wonder... Your mother wouldn't happen to still be in the area, would she?"

"My mother? Yes, she's got a condo in town now."

"Great. I'll look forward to talking with her soon. Any chance I could get you to give me her phone number?" He flipped the notebook open again.

"Sorry, Detective. I don't usually give out my mom's number to strange men."

He didn't seem overly concerned or insulted that she'd called him a strange man. Instead, he just chuckled and gave her another smile. "That's all right. I'm sure I can find her. But how about you? Do you give out your number?"

She met his eyes and was amazed to find the slightest hint of amusement. Was he enjoying her frustration? It certainly seemed so. Well, she wasn't enjoying it. Maybe he thought it was great fun to accuse her father of murder, but she didn't much care for his style of entertainment. No matter how good he looked in that suit, she was not playing along.

"If you need me, call my office," she said, rising from the pew where she'd been sitting. "My assistant can set up an appointment."

"Very well." He made another note. "I'll keep you posted on what we find."

"Yes. Please do that."

With a toss of her head, she pulled her purse up onto her shoulder and strode down the aisle toward the front door. Her nerves were more frazzled than ever, and now she was angry, as well. Who did this Detective TJ Douglas think he was, coming here and assuming he could peg her father with murder? It was all she could do to keep walking away from him and not turn back to give him a piece of her mind.

Some detective he was. He didn't even know who was buried out there behind the church, and already he thought he had solved the crime. Whoever that poor soul was, he had no connection to her father—Carlie knew *that* beyond a doubt.

The discovery of a body here did cause additional problems beyond these false accusations, though. Her request for a bank loan would obviously be put on hold. As much as she wanted to claim this discovery had nothing to do with her, she was neck deep in it. Her finances, her faith, her future, her feelings…she was all tied up in this, and her head was spinning.

Worse, she knew the next thing she had to do would be even harder than finding a body. She had to go tell her mother about this. Conversation there was strained, even on the best day. This was *not* the best day.

Chapter Three

TJ watched Carlie Fenton march out of the church, her shoes clicking on the dusty wood floor. He really couldn't blame her for being angry with him. It must've been hard to hear his questions, to relive that time in her life. It must've been even harder to answer him. She knew as well as he did that if this body did turn out to be Ricky LeMaster, she'd given TJ reason to make her father his prime suspect.

At the same time, she was clearly convinced that whatever crime had been committed, her father was not involved. Her answers had seemed truthful; TJ hadn't detected any obvious deception. Then again, he'd only just met the woman and really had no idea how to read her. Just because she had a pretty face and big, earnest blue eyes didn't mean he should trust her. He'd learned that too many times in the past.

She had chewed her bottom lip four times—he'd counted. He couldn't decide if that was just a nervous habit or if she was struggling to choose her words carefully. Her gaze had darted around the room, stopping

most frequently on the places where—he assumed—
her father had often been. Was she mourning him? Pro-
tecting him?

Her uneasiness was obvious. Most people had some
level of anxiety when he talked to them. That was just
the nature of his job. With Carlie Fenton, it was simple
to explain her anxiousness—she had practically stum-
bled into a hole with a corpse, after all.

But was she telling him all that she knew? Overall,
it seemed she'd been open with him, despite her obvious frustrations. In his line of work, he'd learned a few
things about judging people's reactions. As he'd questioned Carlie, he'd studied her expression, her body lan-
guage, her choice of phrases. From what he could see,
the young woman's shock and horror at finding that
body were genuine. The story she'd told him was be-
lievable, and her loyalty to her father was unwavering.

That was the part that caused him some worry. She
was so determined to defend the memory of her father
that he worried she might hold back pertinent details.
Whomever that body in the dirt belonged to, it was obvious it had been there for years. Like it or not, Carlie's
father had more reason to know about it than anyone
else, given his position here. And Carlie was TJ's clos-
est link to the man. Their conversation might be done
for now, but it was far from over.

Of course, identity still needed to be verified, so it
was premature for TJ to assume the victim was Ricky
LeMaster. The fact that the men on-site had all jumped
to the same conclusion was definitely worth noting.
Carlie's reaction to that conclusion was also worth noting—she'd hardly flinched when Ricky's name came

up. While TJ was sure she hadn't expected to find the body there, the idea that it was her old boyfriend didn't entirely shock her. Why would that be the case if she really had believed he'd run away? TJ was going to be very interested in her explanation.

He checked his watch. For now, the crime scene team was on-site and they had work to do. He needed to co-ordinate with them.

Giving Carlie enough time to huff away from him, he took a moment to appreciate his surroundings. The sanctuary must've been quite comfortable when it was in use; it was large enough to seat a couple hundred congregants yet still small enough to feel friendly. He could easily imagine the atmosphere on a Sunday morning. People sharing smiles, greeting each other, asking after family members, and children laughing in the aisles. He knew that place. He also knew the emptiness when that place stopped being a comfort and a haven. As Carlie had said, it just didn't quite seem like *home* anymore.

Church hadn't felt like home to TJ for quite a few years. Usually that didn't bother him—he could forget it altogether. Today, though, here he was, sitting in a pew, wondering if the preacher's daughter had anything to do with a murder.

Well, it wouldn't be the first time his job had led him to church. But this time would be different, he promised himself. This time, he would see that the victim found justice.

Carlie focused on the road as she drove back into town. She'd made her hasty retreat from that nosy detective, made plans to meet with the bank appraiser later this week and left Epiphany Church as fast as she could. It took extra effort to keep her car's speed at the legal limit. She wished she could leave Melfield altogether, forget this day had ever happened.

She couldn't, of course. There was no avoiding what had to be done. Her mom needed to know about this, and it would be far better coming from Carlie than from Detective Douglas.

Her mother's tidy condo sat in a new development just on the outskirts of town. After living in a parsonage for most of her married life, she hadn't quite known what to do when she was widowed. The first place she'd moved to was a small apartment. Most of the family belongings had gone into storage.

Carlie had worried for her mom at first, but she'd had school to focus on, then starting her career. Plus, she'd had her own grief to work through. Her mother never had been one to give in to emotion—she never let Carlie see how she felt, and she certainly didn't encourage Carlie to share her own feelings. So their relationship had become cool, distant and awkward.

Her mom had seemed interested only in work back then. She got a job at the local hospital and pushed Carlie to excel, to get a good job of her own and to ignore the huge, empty spot in her soul that had been left after her dad's passing. It was as if their whole lifetime of living was suddenly to be forgotten, ignored. Old family photos were locked up, buried in boxes of dishes, knickknacks and useless memorabilia. The life Carlie had known seemed to have ended the day her father died.

But now all of that old existence would have to be revisited. Her mother wouldn't like it—Carlie knew that much, for sure. What she didn't know was what her mother might have to say about it all. Carlie wasn't certain she wanted to hear.

Arriving at the condo complex, she was glad she'd made the choice not to call first. She parked her car, took a deep breath and headed up to knock at the door. A decorative wreath made of vines and silk flowers hung there in welcome. A shiny blue pot with bright red geraniums sat at the corner of her mother's little porch. Two white rocking chairs waited for company to stop by and chat.

Carlie flexed her fingers, building up the strength to knock. It sounded weak, just the same. She heard her mother's footsteps from inside. The door opened in a moment.

"Carlie! I didn't know you were coming by today. Did we have plans?"

"No, Mom. I just… I just dropped by."

Her mother ushered her in, always the perfect hostess as long as you didn't want to talk about anything important. The condo was bright and airy with pleasant decor and picture-perfect furnishings. Nothing was familiar—all the old things were still in storage. Her mom had started fresh when she'd moved into this place just over a year ago. She loved it, so Carlie pretended to, as well.

"Can I get you some tea?" her mother offered. "I just put a pitcher in the fridge."

"Yeah, actually. I could use something to drink."

She dropped her purse on a chair and followed her mother into the kitchen. Mom did make awfully good iced tea. It would help the dry feeling in the back of

Carlie's throat, although she knew that had nothing to do with being thirsty.

"So, what have you been up to today, honey?" her mom asked as she gathered two tall glasses and added ice cubes.

"Well...that's why I'm here, actually. I was out at the church."

"Oh? Was today that businesswomen's brunch? I thought that was next week."

"No, Mom, not the new church. I was out at *our* church, at Epiphany."

Her mother's movements became noticeably stiff. "Don't tell me you're still thinking about buying that place! You already found a nice little office to lease for your business, so you don't need that musty, old church building. Besides, I thought the bank turned down your loan."

"I told you about it, Mom. They didn't turn me down. They just said we needed to do some work to find out how much it will actually cost to fix the problems with the foundation."

"Your father got that repaired years ago."

"No, he didn't. That's sort of the issue. It never really got fixed and...well... We brought in a backhoe, and today, they found something there."

Was her mother making an extra effort not to face her, or did it really take this long to pour iced tea?

"Found something? What do you mean?"

"They found a body, Mom. Someone was buried there!"

"You mean they dug into the cemetery? But that won't fix anything."

Carlie sighed. She knew her mother's way of intentionally not understanding something she didn't like. Hearing about a body buried next to Epiphany Church would definitely qualify.

"No, I'm pretty sure that's not what this is," she explained carefully. "The detective assured me he's going to look into that possibility, but it really looked like—"

"Detective?"

"Yes, some new guy named Douglas."

"TJ Douglas! Oh, he's very nice."

"You know him?"

"From church, of course. His brother is the minister at Faith Community so he attends there occasionally."

This took Carlie by surprise. "His brother is the minister there?"

"Oh, yes! Pastor Matt was so excited when he announced about six months ago that TJ was coming to Melfield, joining the sheriff's office. He's awfully good-looking, don't you think?"

"Yes… I guess so, but Mom! Did you hear what I said? They uncovered a body at Epiphany Church, buried right near the foundation. Detective Douglas started investigating, and the guys on the work crew…they suggested that maybe it was Ricky."

"Ricky?"

"You remember Ricky LeMaster."

"Oh! That troubled boy who went missing. Your father always said he felt guilty about that."

Carlie nearly choked on her surprise. "What do you mean, he felt *guilty* about that? What did he possibly have to feel guilty over?"

"He felt bad about being too hard on the boy. He really did try to help him, though. They met together several times, there at the church. You remember."

"No, not really. I mostly remember them having words in the parking lot that day."

Her mother's memory seemed to be more complete. "Oh, your dad regretted his harsh words. He called the boy to come talk with him."

"I don't recall much about that. What happened?"

"Your father became frustrated. Seems that boy just had so much anger inside him. Your father couldn't get through to him. He tried to offer counsel, help him get into college, even hired him for some odd jobs at the church. It didn't last long, though, and that boy just left town. We never heard from him again."

Carlie rubbed her temples—she was starting to get a headache. How had she not known her father was so involved with Ricky after that day? It made sense, though. Dad would've never wanted to leave things unresolved. Of course he would have tried to talk to Ricky, to apologize for losing his cool and to help the boy deal with his anger. But why didn't she have any memories about this?

And what would Detective Douglas think if he knew about it now? He might decide it sounded like just more opportunity for her father to be a part of something awful. It was probably a good thing Carlie hadn't remembered it when she was babbling back in the sanctuary. The less connection her father had with Ricky, the less reason that eager detective would have to posthumously convict him.

So, he was the brother of Rev. Matt Douglas from Faith Community Church in town, was he? She found that hard to believe—Pastor Matt was friendly and warm, and he had a real heart for outreach in the area. As much as Carlie tried to resent that congregation for absorbing the membership of Epiphany and being a big part of her father's legacy getting lost, she had to admit Matt was a nice guy. Too bad his brother was manipulative, overly suspicious and asked intrusive questions.

Carlie had just taken the first sip of her iced tea when there was a knock at the front door. Her mother jumped. Carlie craned her neck to see past the kitchen doorway toward the little entry hall. The lace curtains over the broad front window provided just enough of a view that she could see the back end of a sheriff's car in the driveway. Through the fan-shaped window in the front door, she could see the top of a man's head, too. She recognized that unruly dark hair right away.

"Don't answer it!" she hissed at her mother.

But her mother was already drying her hands and heading toward the door. "Nonsense. It looks like someone from the sheriff's office. I have to answer it."

Carlie grabbed her mother's arm and stopped her as she passed. "Mom, listen. Please…don't mention to Detective Douglas about Dad's meetings with Ricky, especially if he got upset or frustrated by them. Okay?"

"It's Detective Douglas? Well, what a small world. I'll invite him in. Pour him some tea, Carlie. It's getting warm out there."

Carlie's head pounded. Things were getting warm in here, too.

Chapter Four

TJ hadn't been surprised to see Carlie's car parked in her mother's driveway. He'd watched her drive off in it, leaving the old church parking lot in a cloud of dust. She'd been upset, and he knew his blunt questioning had done nothing to ease the shock she must have felt. It only made sense that she would go rushing to her mother.

Naturally, she'd want to be with someone she trusted and cared about after the experience she'd had. Anyone would feel that way, and Carlie must be glad to have her mother so close by at this time. He felt a twinge of guilt to be disturbing them now.

But he had a job to do. No matter how shocked Carlie had seemed about that body next to her dad's church, he couldn't assume her reaction was authentic. People could be very good actors sometimes—he'd certainly been fooled more than once. So far, the only lead he had was Carlie's family's connection to this. Maybe she and her mother really didn't know anything, as she had convincingly told him already, but maybe they did.

Possibly she had run to her mother for more than just moral support. TJ didn't like being suspicious of everyone, but that was what made him a good detective. Carlie might have wanted to come cry on her mother's shoulder, or she might have rushed over to give her a warning, to make sure they had their stories straight.

Like it or not, the dearly departed Reverend Fenton was TJ's prime suspect in what would almost certainly turn out to be a murder. What had really happened between him and the young delinquent? How much did his widow and daughter know about it?

TJ wanted to believe Carlie was nothing more than an innocent bystander, that she was as clueless and uninvolved in this as she claimed. But was she? He needed to approach Carlie Fenton as he would any possible suspect, despite this unexpected instinct to trust her.

So here he was, following her to her mother's front door. Carlie would probably not be happy to see him. Would her mother have any useful information to add to what Carlie had told him? Every clue he could get was important before this case got any colder.

He hadn't even knocked when the door opened and a smiling middle-aged woman greeted him. He recognized her from church, but he wasn't sure if they'd ever been introduced. Probably they had. His brother took his role as pastor very seriously. Matt knew every one of his parishioners by name and had done his best to introduce TJ to all of them when he'd moved here to Melfield six months ago. It had been exhausting. TJ certainly did not envy his brother's career path. Dealing with the dead was much easier than dealing with the living.

"Detective Douglas!" the woman exclaimed with a ready smile.

Apparently, they *had* been introduced. "Good morning, Mrs. Fenton. I—"

"Oh, call me Eileen," she said, gesturing warmly and pulling the door wide. "Come in, come in! Carlie just told me that she'd met you today. How nice of you to drop by."

"Well, I was… Um, do you have a few minutes to talk?" he said, still standing on the porch. "I suppose your daughter explained what was discovered today at the old church."

Maybe the woman hadn't heard him, but she showed no reaction to his mention of the discovery. She simply kept smiling and inviting him inside. He hadn't expected such a gracious welcome and was a bit caught off guard by it. Had Carlie not told her what had happened? The fact that Mrs. Fenton showed such little interest in the discovery of a dead body was notable, to say the least.

"I was actually hoping you might have some details to add. Do you remember anything from that time, just before the LeMaster boy disappeared?"

"So they've identified him for sure already?" she asked. "Carlie said you suspected that's who it might be."

"Well, it will be some time before there's a positive ID, but since this is the direction things are pointing in, I'm trying to get on top of it."

"You detectives don't waste much time, I guess. But have a seat. Carlie, did you get some tea for our guest?"

Mrs. Fenton practically pushed him into the kitchen.

Carlie was there and she was glaring at him. This was definitely more like the welcome he'd expected.

"Hello again, Miss Fenton," he said.

She shoved a glass of iced tea toward him. "Here. My mother makes the best tea."

He took the glass and assumed that since the elder Fenton lady had made it, he could trust that it was safe to drink. If Carlie had made the tea for him, he wasn't sure he would be so eager to give it a try. The anger flashing in her eyes warned him that she might have considered adding something special to the brew.

"Thank you," he said, taking a cautious sip. "Yes, it is very good."

"The secret is my little herb garden out back," Mrs. Fenton replied. "I always keep fresh peppermint and a pot of chamomile growing. Sometimes, I bring home a fresh ginger root and grind that up too and steep it in my hot tea. It's actually very good for the digestion, you know."

"Mother, I'm sure the detective didn't come here to discuss tea," Carlie said, saving him from a conversation that he knew absolutely nothing about.

Mrs. Fenton nodded. "You're right. I'm sorry, Detective. It really is quite a shock what you found today. Go ahead. What would you like to ask me about it?"

She pulled out a chair at the kitchen table and motioned for him to sit. As encouragement, she took the chair across from him. The iced tea really was very refreshing, and he did appreciate her willingness to talk. Usually he preferred to remain standing—keeping things as professional as possible—but in this instance, it seemed some informality would produce the best results. He seated himself and took another sip before continuing.

Carlie remained standing at the counter, still glaring.

"I just need to know what you remember from the time before Ricky LeMaster went missing," he asked Mrs. Fenton.

She shrugged. "Not much, I'm afraid. Carlie has probably already told you everything we know about poor Ricky."

"Your husband was not too happy with the boy, I take it?"

"That's putting it mildly!" she said with an offhanded chuckle.

Carlie quickly jumped in. "A lot of people had reason to be upset with Ricky during that time."

Her mother went on, oblivious to Carlie's warning glances. "Oh, yes, he did get into some mischief. You should have seen the way he kept pestering Carlie, Detective, after she quit going out with him… It was really uncalled for. All the awful things he said about her! Well, you can imagine how that might make any parent feel. Do you have children, Detective?"

"Er, no. I don't. But Carlie also mentioned there had been some vandalism at the church?"

"It was shocking, yes. The sheriff never could determine who had done it, but Carlie and her dad were convinced it was Ricky. Vance said it was— Oh, Vance was my husband, you know. Vance Fenton. He said the vandalism was the boy's cry for help."

"And did he try to help him?"

"Of course! Not that Ricky was cooperative, but my husband did try to reach that poor boy. He came home one afternoon very encouraged, in fact. He said Ricky had asked him to help fill out some college applications, as I recall. I got the idea that he didn't get a lot of attention at home."

"College applications? So Ricky was planning to go to college?"

Mrs. Fenton shrugged. "I guess so. My husband thought it was a good sign that Ricky was thinking about the future, planning to make something of himself."

"And still no one was suspicious when he just disappeared?"

"He was a troubled boy, Detective. Maybe he couldn't get into those colleges he applied for, or maybe his family just didn't have the money. When he left Melfield—or when we *thought* he left Melfield—it really didn't seem that out of character for him. Even the sheriff decided it was just a case of a runaway teen."

"So the sheriff at that time didn't investigate his disappearance?"

"Oh, yes, he did! Asked my husband a bunch of questions—how upset was he with Ricky, did Ricky ever make any threats against us or himself, when was the last time we saw him…all those questions."

TJ made a mental note. So the previous sheriff had thought Reverend Fenton might have known something about the boy? As much as TJ hated to think badly of a man who'd devoted his life to serving God, he couldn't ignore the evidence that seemed to be presenting itself.

True, he had little information to even begin an investigation. They were still guessing at the identity of the body, and there was no proof so far that a crime actually had been committed. For all they knew, some unknown stranger had fallen into that construction site at the church and become accidentally buried. Ricky LeMaster could still be out there somewhere, happily enjoying his life as a willful runaway.

But from his experience and what he'd seen so far, this case gave every indication of being exactly what it appeared—a murder. The sooner he gathered information, the better chance he'd have of uncovering the truth.

And it was clear Carlie had already begun advising her mother on what—and what not—to say about this matter. TJ was glad he'd come directly here. If he'd waited even a day or two, perhaps Mrs. Fenton would have been convinced to stay silent on what had transpired those dozen years ago.

"I'm afraid we really don't know anything more that could help you," Carlie said firmly. "As my mother said, Ricky had issues. I wasn't the only one he caused trouble for, you know."

"Oh? There were other ex-girlfriends?"

"A couple girls complained about him, yes," Carlie replied.

"And don't forget that trouble with his sister!" Mrs. Fenton added.

TJ was intrigued. "His sister?"

"Oh, yes," Mrs. Fenton said. "He was always bullying her, picking fights with any boys who seemed interested in her."

Now, this was a new angle. TJ was eager to learn more.

"Who were these boys he picked fights with? Would any of them still be in the area? I'd like to talk to them."

"I remember he had a run-in with one of his best friends about it," Carlie said. "His name was Mitchell. But he's not around here anymore. He left town a few years ago. I'm not sure where he went. Sorry."

"But there's that other boy!" Mrs. Fenton chimed in quickly. "He might know. He was good friends with both of them."

Carlie exchanged a look with her mother. "I'm sure he doesn't know anything, Mom."

"Who is this guy?" TJ asked.

"He and Ricky used to run around all the time," Mrs. Fenton said. "And Mitchell, too. They were like the Three Musketeers, always out driving too fast or making too much noise."

"But he hasn't heard from Mitchell in years," Carlie insisted.

"So, he's a friend of yours?" TJ questioned. "I wonder what he'll have to say when we tell him what we found at the church today."

Carlie shrugged. "He seemed as shocked as any of us."

"You talked to him already? You told him about it?"

"I didn't have to," she replied. "He saw for himself. He was there this morning."

"He was *there*? Who is this guy?"

"He's probably a friend of yours," she said, meeting TJ's gaze. "He's Detective David Scheuster."

Carlie could tell her words surprised the detective. She felt an odd satisfaction at that—she had information he needed. If TJ wanted to continue his investigation, he needed her cooperation. To get it, he would have to cooperate with her.

And she was not about to let him keep her father at the top of his suspect list.

"You know, Detective Scheuster's wife is Ricky's sister," she informed him. "I'm sure she could answer some questions for you. And she's a friend of mine."

Well, that was a bit of an exaggeration. Carlie had been friends with Tamara back in high school, but other than seeing her pop up on social media over the years, they hadn't really kept in touch. Not that TJ needed to know that. Carlie was happy to stretch the truth a bit if it kept her in the loop.

"I didn't know that," TJ said with the slightest hint of a nod. "I'd like to find out what she knows about her brother's disappearance."

"If you're going to talk to her, I could go with you," Carlie suggested, but too quickly. She hadn't meant to sound so eager; she just wasn't sure what Tamara might say, and she wanted to be there to hear it.

"No, thank you."

"But she needs to know that we might have found Ricky's body!"

"I'm sure she already does," he replied. "No doubt Detective Scheuster has called his wife to let her know."

"You're probably right," Carlie said. "But she might appreciate having an old friend on hand to—"

"Thank you, Miss Fenton, but I've got this. Unless you feel that Mrs. Scheuster will need a lawyer on hand for any reason?"

"No, of course not! I didn't mean to suggest that she might—"

"Good. Then there's no cause for you to cut short your visit with your mother," he said, giving her a triumphant smile. "I won't take up more of your time. Thank you, Mrs. Fenton, for the tea. It's very refreshing. I'm sorry that today's discovery has undoubtedly dredged up some painful memories for you, but I hope you'll let me stop by again sometime…when you're not entertaining."

Carlie tried not to let her frustration show. Oh, he was smooth, all right. Those green eyes sparkled with deceptive charm. Obviously, he had hoped to talk to her mother without her here. What did he think? Carlie might prevent her mother from telling him? Did he suspect her of harboring all sorts of pertinent information that she might withhold? His polite, gracious demeanor wasn't fooling Carlie one bit.

Her mother, on the other hand, seemed to gobble it up.

"Drop by anytime, Detective," the woman said, practically swooning under TJ's spell. "If I know to expect you, I'll whip up one of my famous blackberry stack cakes."

Now she was ready to bake for the man! Her mom hadn't made one of her stack cakes for Carlie in ages. She rolled her eyes. Just because the detective was new in Melfield and admittedly attractive did not excuse her mother's fawning. It was embarrassing.

TJ didn't seem to mind, though. He just smiled as if he was used to such adulation. Probably he was.

"It sounds delicious, Mrs. Fenton, but there's no need for that. I only have a few questions to go over with you, just formalities. Right now, though, I should probably meet with Mrs. Scheuster."

"Of course…of course," her mother said, obviously ready to agree with anything the detective said.

He'd probably use the same tactic on Tamara—dazzle her with his smile and then charm her into saying whatever he wanted to hear. Carlie cringed inside to think what that might be. No doubt TJ would ask her all about Ricky's feelings toward Carlie's dad…what things he might have said about him in their home. There was no telling what lies Ricky had told his family back then to cover for his bad behavior. He could've made her father out to be a ranting ogre, and TJ would hear all about it.

"I really should go with you," Carlie tried again. "I know where they live, over in that new development behind the high school. I don't recall the address, but I could show you the house."

"Thanks, but I've got to go back out to the crime scene and make sure things are secure there. I'll have my detective take me to meet with his wife."

For one crazy moment, Carlie tried to think of a way to convince him to take her, but her mom put an end to any hope of that. She patted the detective's broad shoulder and had the nerve to apologize.

"Don't mind her, Detective. Carlie's a lawyer, you know. She loves all this legal stuff—fact-finding and depositions and all that."

"Yes, I know all about lawyers," TJ replied with an extra gleam in his eye directed at Carlie. "I'm sure she is very aware that unhindered investigation is essential for such an important matter as possible murder."

"I assure you I am as eager as anyone to find out what happened to that poor person out there…and to find out who he really is," Carlie said.

TJ nodded, acknowledging her reminder. "I'm glad to hear it. And yes, of course, we can hardly go around making any accusations until we have a positive identification."

"And until we have any actual suspects to accuse," she noted, though she wasn't sure he had heard her.

By now, TJ had made his way to the front door, her mother still fussing over him as she ushered him out. That undefined gleam in his eye lingered as he thanked them both for their time and promised to visit her mother again. Carlie wondered how he'd make certain she wasn't there then, but knew he'd find a way. She'd have to remind her mother to be careful in her description of the friction between Ricky and her dad. Not that they had anything to hide, of course, but there was no need to give TJ any false impressions.

Her mother waved at him as he left, and Carlie watched out the window to make sure he really did get in his cruiser and drive away. Back to the church, he had said. Back to see what else had been dug up in that unexpected grave.

"Such a nice-looking young man!" Mom said with a comical sigh. "You should get to know him better, Carlie."

"I'd rather not know him at all," she grumbled. "You do understand what's going on, don't you? They found a body buried at our old church. It's been there a long time, Mom. Back when Dad was the pastor there, when that digging was being done on the foundation."

"Awful, just awful. I wonder who it really is."

"It's probably Ricky. I got a look at him. Jeans, letterman jacket… It sure could have been Ricky."

"That's too bad. I thought when he sent that postcard a few years ago, it meant he was fine, doing all right in the world."

Carlie nearly spit the iced tea she had just sipped. "*Postcard*? What postcard, Mom?"

Chapter Five

"You know, the postcard Ricky sent to his sister."

"Ricky sent her a *postcard*? When?"

"Oh, about ten years ago, I guess."

"But that was well *after* he disappeared!"

Carlie tried to think back to that time. Had she heard about this? She would've been a senior in high school around that time, planning for college. Ricky's disappearance had no longer been fresh at that point; she'd been too busy anticipating her future to worry about him. Did she remember anything about a *postcard*? No, she honestly didn't.

"You must remember, Carlie," her mother went on. "We were all pretty excited to hear about it. Seemed like the mystery was solved—he'd run off, just like everyone had thought all along."

"But how could he have? If we found his body today, and it was in a place that hasn't been touched for twelve years… Unless it isn't his body. Could you be wrong about when he sent that postcard? You're sure it was after the work on the parsonage?"

"Well, let's see. I remember we finished up that project on the church foundation just before you turned sixteen. Remember? We had your party at the parsonage, and I was so glad that all the dirt and the big equipment was out of the parking lot finally. It had been such a mess on Easter."

Carlie's birthday was May 5, so if her mother remembered equipment there in April for Easter but gone by her birthday, that narrowed down the window for when the body could have been buried. This was good information.

"Yeah, okay. That rings a bell."

"And remember when Ricky disappeared, everyone talked about how close it was to graduation?"

"Yes, that was the one part that made no sense at all."

"So if he was supposed to graduate in June, he probably didn't even disappear until after that work on the foundation was done, maybe after your birthday sometime."

"I guess that could be true. But what about this postcard? Are you sure that's when it arrived?"

"I think so. It was just before the LeMaster girl was getting married. What was her name?"

"Tamara. She's Tamara Scheuster now. But tell me about the postcard!"

"Everyone was talking about it. She was so happy. One day, a postcard just arrived at their house, addressed to her, and it was from Ricky. I guess he heard about her getting engaged and he wished her well."

"Where was it sent from?"

"Oh, I don't remember. We were all just happy to know he was out there somewhere, doing okay. The sister especially. She didn't even want to get married without her brother, but that postcard from him helped her feel better, I guess. One of my Bible study ladies worked with the girl's mother, and that's how I heard so much about it."

"I can't believe I don't remember any of this."

"Well, you were pretty busy with your own life, and no one really thought anything bad had happened to Ricky. Why would a simple postcard seem so memorable?"

"I should have cared a little more, though. But if Ricky sent his sister a postcard a year and a half after this body was buried at the church, it can't be Ricky we found today!"

"It must not be," her mom agreed. "And I'm glad. Your father had such high hopes for him, despite all the trouble."

"But don't you see? The detective is going to talk to Ricky's sister now. What do you think she'll have to say about Dad? I don't imagine Ricky had a lot of nice things to say about him. What if he told his sister lies and she repeats them to the detective? He'll drag Dad's name through the mud for no reason."

Her mother actually paused to consider this. "Hmm, I suppose there might have been lies. Ricky never did take credit for his own bad behavior, always blaming everyone else. But you know your father was a good, decent man, Carlie. Everyone will say so. It won't matter if Ricky told his sister some silly falsehoods. No one will believe them."

"TJ might." Carlie tried not to be pessimistic, but she'd seen too many victims be let down by the law.

"And whether Ricky is living happily-ever-after in Louisville or anywhere else, the fact remains that there has been a body buried at Epiphany Church. People are going to wonder who knew about it."

News of this discovery was going to spread fast. There would be a lot of pressure on TJ to solve the case quickly. It was bound to be in the front-page headlines of the local paper every day until they had answers. Anyone TJ investigated would be public knowledge—it was impossible to keep things like that quiet in a small town. If there was even a hint of suspicion on anyone, people would not soon forget it, even if that suspect was a good, decent man.

If Ricky had maligned her father and then Tamara repeated that to TJ, Carlie's dad would become part of the investigation. His name would be irrevocably smeared. Investigators could simply identify the body, find some connection to the reverend and call the case closed. There would be no trial, no chance for her dad to be absolved and no hope of finding the real killer. TJ could wash his hands of it and walk away, looking like a hero.

She'd seen it happen before. Too many times.

"I'm sure Ricky's sister hardly remembers anything about your father," her mother said, shaking her head and going back into the kitchen. "But, oh, maybe I should call the sheriff's office and have them get in touch with Detective Douglas. He should probably know that this can't be Ricky LeMaster, don't you think?"

"Um, yeah. But don't call the office. He told us where he's going, right? I'll just run out and catch him, let him know."

Her mom smiled. "That's a much better idea. You should absolutely go tell him about this."

Carlie felt just a twinge of guilt as she returned her mother's smile. Her mother thought she knew what Carlie was up to, that she was eager for another chance to see the handsome new detective. Well, she wasn't quite right. Carlie would be seeing the detective again—and she would make sure he knew about the postcard from Ricky—but first Carlie hoped to see someone else. She wanted to hear what Tamara had to say about it herself.

There should just be enough time. TJ was going out to the old church before he and the other detective came back into town to talk to Tamara. Well, that would give Carlie the chance to speak with her first. Yes, she and Ricky's sister really ought to do some catching up.

And Carlie could find out just what her old friend *did* remember about Ricky's disappearance...and what Ricky had said about her father.

TJ left the stucco and brick cul-de-sac where Mrs. Fenton's condo complex was and pulled his cruiser out onto the main road back into Melfield. He'd have to go through town, then head north to return to Epiphany Church. Dispatch assured him a team was still on-site, so he would check on their progress and connect with Detective Scheuster there.

He supposed he shouldn't read anything into Scheuster not mentioning that his wife was their supposed victim's sister. They had no positive ID yet, so there was no legal reason for the detective to disclose his relation to their potential victim at this point. Once a positive ID was in, then they could decide how closely Scheuster should work on the case.

He only hoped he wouldn't get too much interference from Carlie. She obviously had a vested interest—naturally she would want to know what he was finding. Would she step back and let him do his job? With her father's good name on the line, he highly doubted it.

Not that he could entirely blame her. Clearly she'd put her father on a pedestal. By all accounts, he was a well-respected man here in Melfield. It would be a shame to see that image come crashing down, should TJ uncover information to implicate him.

Carlie would likely be devastated; TJ hated what his investigation might ultimately do to her. He took no joy in suspecting a man of God, but what choice did he have? The few clues he had found so far seemed to lead directly to Carlie's father. TJ couldn't let the determined attorney get under his skin and deter him from his efforts.

He had just pulled to a stop at the red light on Main Street when his phone buzzed. Switching on the handsfree, he answered. His brother's energetic voice greeted him.

Somehow news had already reached Matt about the discovery at Epiphany Church.

"Yes, it's true we found a body out there," TJ confirmed. "And good morning to you, too."

"But is it this Ricky boy people are talking about?" Matt asked, skipping right over the usual pleasantries.

"You know I can't tell you that. Even if we did have a positive identification—which we don't—I can't talk about an ongoing investigation. How on earth did you hear about it already?"

Matt laughed. "It's a small town and this is big news. Of course it's traveling fast. I just came into my office and the phone's been ringing nonstop. I'd really like to know what to tell people."

"Tell them a body was discovered and we are investigating. I'm sure the local newspaper will be all over this."

"They are! The reporter doing the lead on this story is in my congregation—he's already hit me up for any insider information I might have."

TJ tried not to sound disgusted. "I hope that's not why you called me. Do people think just because you're my brother you have details about investigations?"

"No, that's not it. I'm their pastor," Matt reminded him. "This is a tragic event and a big shock. People need to know that things are going to be okay, that God's still got it all under control. It's only natural for them to call me for reassurance."

"Or maybe they're looking for reassurance to soothe a guilty conscience."

"You think one of my parishioners committed murder? Come on, TJ, that's a little far-fetched, even for you."

"That victim at Epiphany Church didn't bury himself, Matt. I'm not accusing anyone of anything yet, but as you said, this is a small town. Somebody knows *something*."

"But murder! That's pretty huge. How long ago do you think it happened?"

"Based on what the contractor on-site today was told,

that area had been undisturbed for twelve years. Carlie Fenton agreed that her father oversaw the work during that time."

"You talked to Carlie?"

"I did."

"And what did you think of her?"

"She's a lawyer."

"I know."

"And she thinks very highly of her father, so you can imagine she wasn't exactly helpful answering questions about him."

"You did *not* accuse Reverend Fenton of being involved in a murder!"

"He had a history of animosity toward the LeMaster kid, and he was the one who shut down work on the… No, you won't get me to talk about this, Matt. There's obviously going to be an investigation, and I will follow the leads where they take me."

"Even if it means tarnishing Reverend Fenton's good reputation? Just think of how that will affect his wife and his daughter."

"I can't think about that. You know what I do, Matt. It's my job to ask the uncomfortable questions, to uncover the secrets that people would rather keep hidden. If feelings get hurt because of it…well, that's when you step in. I represent the law, and sometimes, even good people end up on the wrong side of it. You're the one who gets to deal in mercy and forgiveness."

"Not me, TJ. I just tell people who *is* the One who deals in mercy and forgiveness. Maybe sometime you'll take Him up on it."

"Right now, I've got a dead guy in a hole who could

have used some mercy a dozen years ago. You just tell your people that if anyone knows anything about this, I'd love to talk to them."

He could hear the usual disappointment in his brother's voice. "Sure, TJ. I'll be praying for you. Whoever that poor soul is who spent so many years in a forgotten grave, it's good he's got you on the case. I know you'll get justice for him."

"I hope so. He's waited long enough for it—maybe too long."

"Meaning...you think the person responsible might no longer be with us?"

"Meaning a lot can happen in twelve years. Guilty people tend to trip themselves up over time, unless they aren't around to do that."

"So you *do* suspect Reverend Fenton," Matt said with a sigh.

"I told you I don't suspect anyone yet."

"You suspect *everyone*. Be careful, TJ, okay? Everyone has things to hide, even if they aren't guilty of murder. Make sure you're convicting people for the right crime."

"I don't handle conviction. That's up to the lawyers and the courts."

"And we both know how fond you are of them. Just... go easy on Carlie Fenton. Her father did a lot of good for a lot of people here in Melfield."

"Well, someone did something very bad here in Melfield twelve years ago, and whether she likes it or not, Carlie Fenton has a connection to it. She's just going to have to cooperate with me."

For some reason, Matt seemed to find that statement humorous. "I thought you said you'd talked to her."

"I did. She seemed to resent every minute of it."

"And you think she'll cooperate with *you*? More likely, dear brother, you're going to have to cooperate with *her*."

TJ cringed at his brother's words. "She's probably not going to like the kind of cooperation she'll get from me."

Chapter Six

Carlie studied the houses as she drove through the subdivision. She remembered they lived on Park View Drive... Ah, there it was. The Scheusters' cute little tri-level.

She wasn't really sure how she even knew where they lived. It was true that she and Tamara had been friends years ago, but they hadn't remained close. Tamara had graduated a year ahead of Carlie and got married pretty much right away. Carlie had been focused on getting ready for college. With Ricky gone, the two girls really had nothing in common, and they'd simply drifted apart.

As Carlie pulled up to the manicured curb, she noticed Tamara coming out of the house. Her face was pale and her eyes were red. Tamara slung her purse over her shoulder and moved quickly. Carlie stepped out of her car to call to her but felt a moment's pause. Did she really have a right to interrupt the woman right now, when she was clearly preoccupied and was probably reeling from the devastating news she'd received?

But her former friend noticed her. "Carlie? Is that you?"

"Yeah. Hi, Tamara. I, uh, just came by to see how you're doing."

Carlie left her car. Tamara paused in her driveway next to a beige SUV. She gave a weak smile as Carlie approached.

"I guess you heard what they found?"

"Yeah," Carlie said. "I was there."

Tamara seemed surprised by that. "You were there? Did you…? Is it true, then? It's really Ricky?"

"I don't know. They'll have to do some tests to be sure."

"But it could have been Ricky?"

"I just… I really don't know, Tamara. I'm so sorry."

They were both silent for a few seconds, then Tamara cleared her throat, her voice tight with emotion. "Thanks, Carlie. Seriously, though, who else would it be?"

There was no need to answer. "This has got to be so hard for you."

"I guess I knew I'd get this call someday, but you can never really be prepared for it. I just had to call my parents and tell them. That was hard."

"We can't jump to conclusions, of course. I mean, maybe it's not Ricky. You did get that postcard from him, right?"

"How do you know about that?"

"My mom. She learned about it from a friend at church who knew your mom. She told me Ricky sent you a postcard more than a year after he disappeared. Is that true?"

"Yeah, I got a postcard."

"Then maybe we can't assume that Ricky is... Well, I'm sure your husband told you where the body was found today."

"At the old church, he said."

"That's right, buried in a place that hasn't been disturbed for twelve years."

"Yeah, that's how long Ricky's been gone—since April 17, twelve years ago."

"You remember the date?"

"Of course! You don't forget the day your older brother just...isn't there."

"But if he sent you a postcard more than ten years ago..."

Tamara seemed to consider this. "Then he couldn't have already been there at the church. Maybe this isn't Ricky."

"I don't know how it could be. Where did he send that postcard from?"

"All the way across the state, from Fort Samuel. But my parents went there. They tried everything and still couldn't find him. There was just no sign of him."

"Just because he mailed a postcard from there doesn't mean he stayed in the area. But it does mean he was there *after* the work at the church here was finished."

"So what should I tell my parents? I just called them and said to expect the worst."

"I wish I knew what to say, Tamara. It's such a big shock. I can't imagine what you and your family are feeling right now. Can you remember anything else, anything at all about the days around his disappearance?"

"No, I've tried for years to think of any details that might give us some clues. He just…he just left with no warning. All I know is what everyone knows. Dave and their friend Mitch were with Ricky the last night anyone saw him. The next day, he was gone."

"They were with him?"

"Yeah, the three of them had been out partying. They ended up driving around in the church parking lot, goofing off."

"At Epiphany Church?"

"Yes. It was late, but they woke up your dad. He came out and yelled at them to go home, so they did. Ricky was pretty drunk, so one of the guys drove him home. But he must have gotten back in his car and taken off again. They found his car over in Friendsburg a couple weeks later. It was banged up, but there was no sign of him. I don't remember much else… It was a pretty bad time."

"Everyone was stunned by it. But do you remember what—"

Tamara looked away, distracted by the sound of a vehicle approaching the house. Carlie glanced around to see a sheriff's cruiser slowing to turn into the driveway. TJ was at the wheel. He had Scheuster with him.

"Hey, babe, I'm so sorry!" Scheuster said as he jumped out of the car and jogged toward his wife.

Carlie braced for a fight. She caught TJ's gaze as he got out of his car. He was not happy to see her here. His expression said that he had every intention of chastising her for involving herself in his case.

"I really hated to have to call you with the bad news

today," Dave said as he put his arm around Tamara and gave a comforting squeeze.

"But are you sure it's Ricky, hon?" Tamara asked. "I mean, the coroner is going to do an autopsy, isn't he?"

"Of course," Dave assured her. "But we're pretty certain that—"

"What about the postcard?" Carlie injected.

TJ glared at her. "Postcard?"

"How do you know about that?" Dave asked.

"Lots of people know about it," Tamara said, saving Carlie from explaining. "Mom was so excited when that first postcard came from Ricky. She was running around telling everyone in town."

"There was a *postcard*?" TJ asked again, having the very same reaction Carlie had had when her mother mentioned it. "When was this?"

"About a year and a half after Ricky went missing," Carlie said.

TJ glared at her again and then turned his attention back to Tamara. "When was it sent?"

"In early September," Tamara replied. "Well over a year after Ricky was gone. It came just before Scheuster and I got married, addressed to me."

"In your brother's own writing?"

She shrugged. "It sure looked like Ricky's sloppy handwriting."

"I'd like to see this postcard," TJ said.

Tamara adjusted her purse and leaned into her husband. "I don't know… I'm not sure where it is, if I still have it."

"You don't know if you even kept it?"

"We moved a couple times. You know how it is—stuff gets lost," she replied.

"Okay, but you said it was the *first* postcard you got from your brother. There have been more?"

"No, I didn't mean to say it like that. I meant, it was the first postcard he'd ever sent me. I only got one from him."

"Almost a year and a half after that hole was filled in at the church," TJ clarified.

"So it can't be Ricky, can it?" The tiniest glimmer of hope shone on Tamara's face.

Carlie nodded, eager to hear TJ admit that he'd jumped to conclusions too fast and that all his suspicions against her father were completely unfounded. He didn't, though. He just scowled at Scheuster.

"Show her."

The other detective sighed and reached into a pocket. He pulled out a small plastic bag with writing on it in black marker. There was something inside—something small and metallic.

"What is that?" Tamara asked.

"I'm sorry, Tam," Scheuster said as he held the bag out toward her. "They found this on the body."

Tamara reached for it quickly. Too quickly, in fact. Her fingers fumbled and the bag slipped away, dropping directly at Carlie's feet. She stooped to collect it, able to see the object inside through the clear plastic. She held it just for a moment, feeling its heft and mesmerized by what she saw.

Ricky's class ring. The heavy shape with its blue gemstone and carved graduation year was as familiar as if she'd just seen it last week. Carlie had worn that ring for three months on a chain around her neck, proudly showing it off to her friends as a badge of honor that a popular upperclassman had taken an interest in her. She knew the ring would be easy to identify. A quick tilt of the bag and she could confirm: his initials were etched into the silver.

"Is that Ricky's ring?" Tamara said, her voice choked with emotion.

"I recognize it," Carlie said, handing her the bag.

"I'm so, so sorry, babe," Scheuster said, slipping an arm around his wife. "I recognized it, too. His initials are there, just on the inside."

"Don't open the bag," TJ cautioned as Tamara's fingers smoothed over the edges and traced the contours of the ring. "It's evidence, and I've got to get it back to the office. We just thought you ought to know. The coroner still needs to take a look, but I'm pretty confident this is your brother."

Tamara nodded, and gave the bag back to TJ. Her gaze was downcast—any sense of hope seemed to have drained from her. Obviously this was the news she and her family had been dreading for twelve years. Carlie felt the sting of her own emotion. She knew exactly how it was to have the world crumble around you with the sudden news of a lost loved one. For a moment, all the questions surrounding Ricky's death didn't matter. Only a woman's grief.

"If there's anything my mom and I can do for you, Tamara," Carlie offered. "Do you need someone to stay with the kids?"

Tamara shook her head. "No, I'm going to pick them

up now and we're heading out. We need to go to my parents. They live close to Lexington now."

"I'd heard they'd moved a few years ago. Please tell them I... I'm just really sorry for you guys."

"Thanks," Tamara said quietly.

"I should take her now, sir," Scheuster said.

TJ nodded. "Yes, go ahead. I'll let you know if we learn anything more."

Carlie and TJ took a couple steps back to let Dave usher his wife into their SUV. She seemed dazed, as if the full weight of today's horrible discovery was only now truly sinking in. The detective was obviously distressed. He clearly cared about his wife and what she was going through. On top of it, Ricky had been his best friend. It was all so very sad.

Without speaking, Carlie waited with TJ on the Scheusters' sidewalk until the vehicle pulled away. She was sure TJ would have something to say about finding her here, clearly involving herself in this case when he had warned her not to. She was careful not to look at him, not to let those perceptive green eyes skewer her with guilt.

He didn't scold her, though. When he spoke his words were more directed at himself than at her.

"I should have asked her where that postcard was sent from," he muttered.

"Fort Samuel," she replied.

"Fort Samuel, Kentucky? How do you know about that?"

"She told me. I'm familiar with that area because there's a retreat center there where my father used to go a couple times a year for conferences and events."

"Your father used to go there?"

"Sure. There was a group of other ministers who would… Oh, now wait a minute! You're not thinking my father had anything to do with that postcard, are you?"

"Should I be?"

"No! I can't believe you'd even suggest such a thing!"

"I didn't. You did," he noted with a smug grin.

"I most certainly did not. I only told you about the postcard Tamara got because it, well, because…"

"Because you thought it absolved your father," TJ finished for her. "If that hole at the church was closed up and untouched for more than a full year before Ricky sent that postcard, your father couldn't have put him there. And yet, there he is."

It was true—they had the class ring to prove it. But how could it be? Carlie was thoroughly perplexed. "But if Ricky was in Fort Samuel more than a year after he disappeared, then how could his body end up at the church?"

"Exactly. Quite a mystery we have here."

"Well, I'm sure there's a solution. That class ring is not the same as positive identification."

"You're right. We won't be announcing anything about identity until we have the coroner's report and can be certain. Incidentally, you won't be mentioning that ring to anyone. Got it? This is an ongoing investigation."

"I know the rules."

"Do you? I wasn't sure, since I just found you here questioning the victim's sister."

"She's a personal friend of mine, and I have every right to reach out to her."

"How kind of you. Your only reason for rushing over was compassion."

"Yes, I care about her. And my mother did mention the bit about the postcard, so I thought I'd see what Tamara had to say about it."

"Of course."

"And it's a good thing I did. Really, Detective, I don't think she even remembered it with all the shock of the day. If I hadn't been here to bring it up, you wouldn't even know about it now."

"Believe it or not, I'm pretty good at my job," he assured her. "I would have found out about it."

"Eventually. But it would have taken some time."

"Not too much time."

"Some time."

"A short time."

"Oh, for crying out loud. Just admit that I helped you."

"All right, you helped."

She felt far more triumphant than she should have for dragging that slight hint of a compliment from him. Unfortunately, her sense of achievement was short-lived.

"But you're forgetting the downside," he said, dropping the evidence bag with the ring into his pocket.

"And that is…?"

"That postcard could be a pretty incriminating piece of evidence if we find that your father just happened to be away at one of those conferences when the postcard was sent."

Carlie's muscles tightened up and down her spine. She had an idea where TJ was going with this but needed to hear him admit it. "Why on earth would my father mail Tamara a postcard?"

TJ shrugged. The day was warming up by now, but he still wore his dark suit. Nothing seemed to ruffle his composure—not the sun beating down, not Carlie's frustration with his insinuations and not the knowledge that his words of suspicion against her father might undo a lifetime of service and dedication.

"Sending that postcard might have seemed like a very good idea to someone who knew Ricky was dead. What better way to create a distraction or cover their tracks? If people were off looking for Ricky on the other side of the state, they'd be less likely to hunt for a murderer here at home."

Chapter Seven

TJ watched anger take over her expression. Somehow, even that was a good look on her—but of course he couldn't let himself notice. The fact that Carlie Fenton was smart, bold and gorgeous shouldn't make any difference to him at all; she was connected to this case, and he needed to tread carefully with her.

"My father is *not* a murderer!" she declared.

"Well, someone is, Miss Fenton," he said, deciding to leave before the color in her cheeks glowed any hotter. "I've got to get this evidence back to the office."

She followed him to his car. "I'm not done with you, Detective."

"Oh, I'm done with you. But don't worry. You'll hear from me if I have any more questions."

"What are you going to do, then? Declare my father guilty before the coroner even says if there's been foul play?"

He spared her one last look before he climbed into the cruiser. "Of course not. I'm going to find out where your father was when that postcard was mailed."

"And how will you do that? It's not like either of us can go ask him."

"I'm a detective," he reminded her. "I'll find out where he was."

She glared at him, not the least bit deterred even though he'd used the tone of voice that usually ended conversations.

"Fine," she hissed. "You do what you do. I'll prove that my father had nothing to do with this—whoever that body belongs to and however he got into that hole."

TJ pulled the door shut and ignored her as he reached for his seat belt. He left her with nothing to do but step aside and let him pull the car away from the curb. He watched her in the mirror, still standing there fuming as he drove away. Clearly, his interactions with Carlie Fenton were not at an end.

She was definitely a force to be reckoned with, and he would be careful not to underestimate her. To be honest, he was kind of looking forward to working this case, even if it did mean having to sidestep the interloping lawyer. She would make an interesting challenge.

When he left the city to take this job, he'd been hoping to find a slower pace. He'd seen more than enough crime and cruelty to last a lifetime and was eager to serve the good people of Melfield. A quiet life with quiet people seemed like exactly what he wanted. He'd assumed the worst things he'd encounter would be the occasional break-in or possible drug charges.

However, in the six months he'd been with the sheriff's office, he'd begun to wonder if he'd made a mistake. Life was peaceful and quiet here, that was for sure. Maybe things in this small town were *too* quiet for him, in fact. Maybe he wanted to investigate something more than a random barn burglary or shoplifting at the L&O Market. Maybe he was glad they'd found that body at the church this morning.

Of course he wasn't glad *about* the body. Any murder was tragic and horrible, even if it had happened a dozen years ago. That this one was connected to Epiphany Church and the good man who used to be the pastor there made it even more dreadful. No matter how much TJ might relish the challenge of solving a cold case, he had to acknowledge there would be no happy ending. That poor young man would still be gone, and Carlie Fenton would never forgive TJ for considering her father a suspect.

Still, he had to follow the clues. So far every one of them led directly back to the minister. Like it or not, he was investigating Carlie's father.

Ten minutes later, he swiped his security card and headed to his office. A Google search and a phone call or two should pretty quickly answer the question regarding Reverend Fenton's attendance at any sort of conference held in Fort Samuel in late August or early September eleven years ago. He would also call around to find out where the old church records for Epiphany Church were stored. The info he dredged up might not tell him who had committed murder, but perhaps he could find out who sent that postcard.

Which would be a pretty good indication of who knew about the body buried at the church.

Carlie fumed as she drove back into town. She had a client meeting in a half hour, so she couldn't devote any time to investigating now, but she could at least give her mother a quick call. TJ thought he could easily prove her father's whereabouts when that postcard was mailed. Well, she could, too.

"What are you looking for?" her mother asked when Carlie reached her over the phone.

"Dad's schedules, his agendas," Carlie said, hoping she wouldn't have to give too many details. Mom didn't need to know that TJ was off investigating him even as they spoke. "Dad kept such careful records of everything, and I just thought they might be helpful right now. You know, give us an idea of who was around the church back then and all."

"Hmm, yes…good idea. But I can't talk right now. I'm meeting Bob for lunch."

"Oh. Tell him I said hello," Carlie said. "Where are you going for lunch?"

Her mom had been dating Bob for more than a year now, and Carlie still wasn't sure how she felt about it. He was a nice enough guy and all, but something about him just didn't seem… Well, Carlie had never been able to put her finger on it. Was she just being childish? Did anyone ever feel totally comfortable when their parent started dating someone new? She hadn't said anything, but it was hard not to let her mom hear the discomfort in her voice.

If she noticed, she never let on. "We're going to the club. Phil and Margie are joining us, and we'll play nine holes afterward."

Golfing. She should have guessed. It was Bob's passion. Mom had never golfed in her life, but now she talked like she was an old pro at it. Carlie tried to be supportive—golfing was a healthy activity, wasn't it? And she was glad her mother was enjoying her life... really she was.

So why did her knuckles go white as she clenched the steering wheel at the mention of Bob and golfing again?

"Sounds like a fun afternoon," she said. "Maybe we can meet up later?"

"Absolutely. Come by for dinner, why don't you. I've found this great recipe for Mediterranean tacos I'm dying to try."

Carlie cringed at the mention of that, too. But dinner with her mother would be nice. They could talk, and hopefully, Mom could provide details that might help convince TJ that he was barking up the wrong tree if he thought investigating her father would help him solve a murder.

"Sure, Mom. That sounds good. Six o'clock?"

"Perfect! See you then."

Her mom ended the call before Carlie could even say goodbye. She tried not to feel slighted. Of course she hadn't expected her mother to give up her life and focus only on Carlie just because she'd decided to come back to Melfield, but... Well, it might have been nice if she'd tried to spend a little less time with Bob and a little more time being Dad's widow.

Carlie thought of her father every day, and now this horrible discovery made her miss him even more. If only he was here to help them get to the bottom of this, to stand up for himself and convince TJ that he knew nothing of what had happened. If only he were here to promise Carlie—as he always had—that things were in

God's hands and they could trust Him no matter how bleak it might seem.

Surely, Mom hadn't forgotten him so easily. Surely, even with her new condo, new furniture and new life, she still remembered the way things used to be. Talking about all these memories must have brought up some feelings, some sense of nostalgia. Her mother *must* miss her father just a little bit more than usual today.

Or maybe not. It would be pretty hard for Mom to miss her husband while she was out on the golf course with Bob.

The next morning, TJ clocked in to work an hour early. He'd hardly slept all night, his mind working over the elements of the case. So many pieces seemed to fit perfectly: a boy mistreated a girl and made violent threats with vandalism, the enraged father reacted in a public scene, the boy disappeared shortly thereafter. It would be foolish for any detective not to put two and two together when that boy's body is found on the father's job site.

It would be equally foolish, though, for TJ to take everything at face value. What did he really have, outside of circumstantial evidence? Not much. He'd not had time to fully pursue the postcard lead yesterday, but his gut told him he needed to make that his top priority today.

A quick search yesterday had uncovered the name of the conference facility in Fort Samuel that was often used by church groups. He'd decided to start there, tracing back events from the time period in question and then determining if they would have been the sort of thing Reverend Fenton might have been involved in. The preponderance of reports last evening had kept TJ busy until well after business hours, but this morning, he was determined to dive in right away.

A young deputy passed by TJ's door, then paused to poke his head in.

"Hey, you're in early today. Got any news on that body they found yesterday?"

"Sorry, Porter, no ID yet. I'm not sure when the coroner will be able to determine that or cause of death."

"That's rough. How's Scheuster taking it all?"

"He's gone to his in-laws for a couple days with his wife."

"Good for them," the young man said. "Getting away together might be the best thing. I mean, at least something good might come out of this, right? It's no secret that things haven't been good at home for Scheuster. They've had trouble off and on all along, I guess. It was kind of iffy that they'd even get married to start with."

TJ paused at that information. "Really? I hadn't heard."

"I was still in high school, but I remember people talking. It was a toss-up whether Tamara would marry Scheuster or his buddy Mitch. Yeah, there was always big drama with those three guys—got kind of physical a time or two."

"So where is this Mitch?"

The deputy shrugged. "I don't know. Like I said, I was a few years younger. He's still got family in the area, but I'm not sure where he went."

TJ jotted down a quick note to search out this family. So far, he'd been told those three boys were always together, but now to hear things weren't always friendly between them...clearly he needed to follow that lead. Maybe wherever Mitch was, if TJ could find him, he could fill in some of the blanks surrounding Ricky's disappearance.

"It's just such a sad situation," the deputy went on, shaking his head. "All this time, Ricky's family has been thinking he's alive and they were hunting for him all over the place, when really it was the minister who had him buried by that church all along."

TJ was quick to correct him. "There's no indication the minister was involved in whatever happened there."

"But you're investigating him, aren't you?"

"I'm investigating anyone who might have been involved with that boy."

"And that includes the minister, right? I'm not sure how you plan to get around Carlie Fenton. She's kind of a bulldog where her father is concerned."

"So I've learned. But I can handle her if I need to."

The deputy jumped as someone in the hallway cleared their throat. Carlie Fenton stepped into view in the doorway as the deputy nervously backed out.

"The good news is I don't need any handling," she said. Her voice was clipped, and she looked past the deputy to give TJ an icy glare.

"I—I've got reports to file and need to...do things." The deputy practically staggered backward up the hallway in his hurry to extricate himself from the uncomfortable situation.

TJ just gave Carlie a smile. She was dressed in a fitted linen pantsuit and a blue tailored shirt. Everything about her said business. There was no way he could mistake her presence here for a casual visit.

"Miss Fenton, how nice to see you," he greeted. "Just dropping by to say hello?"

"No, as a matter of fact," she said, marching into his office. "I came by to let you know that I have the name of the facility where my father occasionally attended conferences in Fort Samuel."

"Eastwood Conference and Retreat Center?"

She seemed both surprised and annoyed that he already had the information. "Er, yes. How did you know that?"

"I'm a detective, Miss Fenton."

"Just call me Carlie, okay? I'm not a kindergarten teacher."

"All right, Carlie." He made sure to say her name in an overly familiar way. She bristled but could hardly correct him at this point. Her smugness grated on him, and he was glad for any little thing he could do to return the favor.

"But do you also have proof that my father was not anywhere near Fort Samuel when the postcard was mailed?" she asked. "Because I do."

"All right, let's see it."

"I don't have it with me. It's in my mother's storage unit."

"What is it?"

"My father's calendars and agendas. He always kept very careful records, journaling all his meetings, sermon topics, etcetera. All I have to do is go to the unit and find his agendas from that time period. You'll see he was right here in Melfield on those days."

TJ pushed his chair back and stood. "Great. Let's go get those agendas."

She sputtered. "But I... Well, you don't need..."

"That is why you came here, isn't it? So that I could accompany you to find this valuable evidence and provide proof that it's not been tampered with or obstructed in any way?"

"I don't need to tamper with or obstruct anything to prove my father is innocent of this!"

"Great. Then you won't mind showing me." He grabbed his car keys off the desk where he had tossed them. "Come on, let's go get your proof."

Chapter Eight

Hopping into a police car with TJ wasn't exactly what Carlie had planned for her morning. Mostly, she'd stopped by his office to gloat. And maybe to see if he'd come up with any information she didn't have. Apparently, he hadn't. On one hand, this meant he hadn't found any additional reasons to further suspect her father, but on the other hand, it meant he had no solid reason to start looking elsewhere for a guilty party.

She'd given him basic directions to the storage facility where her mom rented a unit, but now they sat in uncomfortable silence as TJ steered the car around the corner at Maple and Elm. Carlie kept her eyes safely on anything but him. Sitting in such close proximity, it was hard to ignore the confidence and authority that the man radiated.

She tried not to be in any way attracted to that. Just because he was a nice-looking man with a sharp brain and an equally sharp suit did not mean she had to notice things like that about him. And she certainly didn't have to like them! As they drove past Faith Community Church, she decided to distract herself with some small talk.

"So your brother is the minister there?"

"He is," he replied. She'd hoped he might volunteer more, but he didn't.

Well, she'd just try again. "He's been in Melfield six or seven years now, right?"

"Seven."

She nodded. Still he was not doing anything to break the tension between them. Taking a deep breath and pretending not to be annoyed, she went on.

"He came to Faith Community as the youth leader, right?"

"Right. It was his second placement after being ordained."

"Really? Where did he serve before?"

"Another position as youth pastor, at our home church back in Louisville."

Could this be an actual conversation? Perhaps she'd found something they could politely converse about. She felt a slight sense of triumph.

"I didn't realize that. You and your brother grew up in the church?"

"We did. It was a pretty big congregation, too. Our mother worked as the church secretary. You can guess how many hours we had to spend there after school every day, waiting for her to be done making sure all the bulletins were printed and the pews were polished for Sunday."

"I'm guessing she put you to work."

"Absolutely. I still get flashbacks to rubbing those pews every time I smell furniture polish."

"Tell me about it. I was in high school before I realized most of the other kids just attended church and didn't have to practically live there and do all the housekeeping."

"What? The preacher's daughter had to do manual labor? I thought you PKs were like royalty or something."

"You haven't met many preachers' kids, have you? No, my parents expected me to be just as devoted to their ministry as they were."

"No wonder you've been trying to buy the building. What do you plan to do with it anyway?"

She shifted nervously in her seat. "I thought I could build my law practice there. I'm renting space in town right now, but my hope is to expand."

"An old church out in the county seems an odd place for a law firm."

"It's quiet and it's private. Some people who need lawyers don't want a big crowd."

"So you focus on criminal law?"

"Some, yes. Mostly family law."

She glanced over to see him nodding. "They overlap too often, don't they?"

He understood. She should have known that with his background in law enforcement, he would be well aware of the connection between the two. The world was entirely too full of divorces that turned violent, custody battles with threats and even probate cases that involved bold-faced theft and destruction of property.

In practicing law, Carlie had needed to develop keen instincts along with shrewd people skills. As much as she loved helping people sort through some of the hardest times of their lives—divorce, bankruptcy, executing the estate of a loved one—she often felt woefully unprepared to assist with the emotional aspects. People were hurting, and there was only so much she could do for them with a stack of documents and a couple black pens.

"I guess my dream is to include maybe some other services for people who need them. You know, access to social workers...something like that."

"That's actually a very good idea," he said.

She laughed. "Don't sound so surprised."

"I just...is Melfield big enough to support something like that?"

"You mean, do us country folk really have that much trouble that we'd need to pay for lawyers like the big-city people do?"

"You have to admit things are pretty quiet here."

"We just dug up a body yesterday," she reminded him. "Obviously Melfield has crime. Yes, the whole county is very rural, but that's all the more reason people here need help. We don't have the same resources as more populated areas. We still have crime, as well as people struggling with addiction and poverty. Those things often lead to trouble and people need help. I'd love to find a way to assist them."

"That's very noble, but there's not a lot of money in helping people."

"Money?" She couldn't help but stare at him. "If I wanted money, I wouldn't have come back to Melfield."

"I'm pretty sure cash will come in handy while rehabbing that old church building."

She had to reluctantly agree. "True. I've been hoping the bank will work with me on it, but now that we found… Well, I'm not so sure it's going to work out for me."

"You'll go back to the city?"

"I don't know. Maybe I shouldn't have left my job there in the first place."

"Where did you work?"

"Blakely & Burke."

"What? Really?"

"You know them?"

"Yeah. I've run across them a time or two."

The tone of his voice indicated he wasn't a big fan of the prestigious law firm. That intrigued her. He must have encountered them in the course of his career in Louisville. He'd been on the police force there, according to her mother. He'd barely been a detective two years before leaving and coming to Melfield. Carlie hadn't thought anything of that, but now she was curious about his story.

"I started with them as a clerk while I was still in law school," she volunteered. "I was happy to get hired in— for a while, I had dreams of making partner one day."

"Sounds like you were on the right track. What made you leave? Why did you come back?"

"Oh, I missed personal connections. I missed actually making a difference. It was a huge law firm, and I was just a small fish in a big pond, I guess."

"A minnow swimming with sharks."

She decided not to let him know how accurate his analogy was. Her last year with Blakely & Burke certainly had left its mark on her. Everything she had worked for had left her disillusioned. She'd quit the firm when she could no longer be who they expected her to be—when she'd looked in the mirror each day and hadn't liked the person she'd become.

She'd come home hoping to find herself once again. So far, she was just as confused and disillusioned as ever.

"I guess I just got tired of the city," she said, simplifying the topic for her herself as much as for TJ. "I didn't like who I was there, and I couldn't keep up with the crazy pace. I'm used to life in a small town, after all."

"Melfield certainly is that," he said, and she wasn't sure he meant it as a compliment.

"But it *is* my home," she defended. "Why did *you* come here? What made you leave the city for this boring little town?"

"It seemed like a good move at the time. Is this the road I turn on here?"

"Yes, but you didn't answer my question."

"Actually, I did. Are those the storage units up ahead on the left?"

"Yes. Pull up there and I'll get us through the gate."

He did as she instructed. Her mother had given her the security code and she typed it into a little keypad at the front entrance to the facility. The large gate swung open, allowing TJ to drive through.

There were five long rows of buildings, multiple storage units in each. Carlie directed him toward building number five. Oddly enough, there was a car parked in front of the unit.

"That's my mother's car," Carlie said. "What's she doing here?"

"Probably the same thing you were going to do—

find those agendas and check them over to make sure they didn't contain any incriminating information before giving them to me."

"Are you accusing me of withholding evidence?"

"Absolutely not. That's why I came along with you, so that couldn't happen."

"It couldn't happen because there is no incriminating information to withhold. That's why I'm happy to cooperate with you. Come on, let's go see what Mom has dug up."

TJ pulled the car to a stop and Carlie quickly climbed out. She hoped he couldn't see that she was more than a little bit upset. Why on earth had her mother come over here so early in the morning?

When they met up for dinner last night, Carlie had explained what she wanted and her mom had assured her all of Dad's things were carefully boxed up. She'd given Carlie the code and one of the keys to get into the unit. She'd even asked what time Carlie thought she'd come by and then made a big deal out of complaining that this would be too early in the morning for her. So why was she here?

"Mom!" Carlie called as she stepped in through the open doorway.

In the dim light, she could see her mother at the back of the unit, partially hidden behind boxes and a stack of chairs. There was a shuffling and rustling of papers. Carlie heard a book drop.

"Carlie! Oh, you're even earlier than you said."

"Good morning to you, too, Mom. What are you doing?"

Something clattered, and her mother came fully into view, clutching a wobbly lamp. She smiled and carefully steadied the lamp on a stack of nearby boxes, then stooped to pick up the book she'd dropped. It appeared to be one of her dad's old journals. Carlie felt a pang of regret—the last time she'd seen one of those books, it had been sitting on her father's desk, just waiting for him to make another daily notation in it. His attention to detail had been so constant, so much a part of the fabric of their lives. How had she and her mom gone on after he was out of their lives?

Looking around at the furnishings and memorabilia piled up here, Carlie realized her mother clearly hadn't. Her life had not gone on after Dad had died. Her life had died, too. Everything that she was had been boxed up and stored away. No wonder Carlie often felt that her mom was almost a stranger these days. In many ways, she was.

Neither of them were the same people they'd been when her dad was living. With Carlie being away at college most of the time, her mom had done her best to build a new life here, while Carlie had poured herself into building a career. This helped explain why coming back to Melfield hadn't felt as much like coming home as she had expected. The home she had known was stacked here, sealed up in cartons marked with black pen to indicate what life used to be.

The storage unit was about the size of a two-car garage, and it was full. A whole lifetime of things took up a great deal of space. One large overhead door spanned the front of the unit, but it was still closed. Mom had used the main door next to it to enter the space. One of the fluorescent light fixtures hanging from the rafters flickered, sending angular shadows through the jumble of things.

Her mother looked lost and uncomfortable in her surroundings.

"Well, I got to thinking," she said. "Maybe it would be better if I came and helped you, sweetie. I have a better idea where everything is here and... Oh! Hello, Detective Douglas. I didn't realize Carlie would be bringing you along with her."

"I don't think Carlie did, either," TJ said, giving Carlie a quick smile. "But she was nice enough to invite me. So, have we found any of the agendas she mentioned?"

Her mom seemed slightly flustered, but that made perfect sense, considering they'd just surprised her amid all these painful old memories.

"Yes, oh, yes! There is a whole box of them, right over here." Her mom turned back to the corner where she had been.

Carlie followed. Several boxes in this area were open. It seemed all of them contained items from her father's office. Apparently, Mom had saved everything—just had all of it packed up, taped up and stacked up in the back of this unit. All of these things that had been such integral parts of her father's life had been intentionally forgotten for more than five years now. If not for the horrible discovery of that body, they would likely have continued to sit here untouched for another five years and then more years after that.

But the body *had* been discovered, and now these boxes were opened. What would they find in her father's belongings? Would she be able to produce the proof she desperately needed to convince TJ to look elsewhere for the murderer?

* * *

TJ followed Carlie deeper into the storage unit. He was surprised to see so many things—it looked like a whole houseful of furniture, decorations, books, with boxes and boxes of everything else. What was the purpose for all of it? Mrs. Fenton seemed to have a nice setup in her current home, so why would she need to keep all these furnishings here? He supposed there was a story behind it.

Maybe he'd ask Carlie about it, once they were driving back into town. The ride over had been surprisingly insightful. He'd been a bit unfair toward her, he decided. It had been wrong to lump all lawyers into one category and assume that Carlie was just money hungry or seeking prestige. Matt would scold him and remind him that he was not being very gracious.

But TJ hadn't seen a lot of grace in his line of work. He supposed he'd forgotten it still existed. He would remember to give Carlie the benefit of the doubt from now on. She hadn't quite explained what made her leave such an esteemed law firm, but he recognized something in her that he knew in himself—she had conviction. He respected that. Although he had to continue investigating her father, he would be more conscious of how it might affect her.

"We're interested in your husband's schedule around the first week of September, eleven years ago," TJ said when Mrs. Fenton smiled at him.

"I've dug it out for you," she said, holding out a leather binder. "This is his agenda for that year—he kept detailed notes for each day."

"What about his desk calendars, Mom?" Carlie asked. "And his journals?"

"Oh, I don't think he saved any of the desk calendars, dear. But his journals should be over here."

She pointed to another stack of boxes. The top one was already open. TJ moved past Carlie to look inside it.

"He sure did a lot of journaling," he commented, struck by the collection he saw there.

"It made it easy to know what to buy him for Christmas," Carlie said. TJ heard the sadness she tried to hide in her voice as she continued, "Every year, Mom let me pick out a couple nice journals for him—sometimes, I got him silly ones with kittens on them, sometimes, they were classier, with Bible verses or his initials embossed in gold. He said he loved them all. I never remember a time when he didn't keep one on his desk, ready to be filled with his thoughts through the day."

Her mother chuckled at the memory. "Any time you'd do something funny, Carlie, he'd tell me not to let him forget to put that in his journal. And sermon ideas! It seemed like every day he'd see something and say 'That needs to go in a sermon!' So many ideas he had… I really can't believe all those journals fit into one box."

"That could be a big help in piecing together what happened," TJ said. "Would you let me take that carton to go through them, Mrs. Fenton? I can assure you I will keep them safe."

Mrs. Fenton glanced at her daughter. Carlie seemed hesitant to advise her. She looked over to TJ.

"We could say no," she said.

"I could get a court order," TJ reminded her.

"You still wouldn't find anything to connect my father to that death."

"I hope I don't," he replied. "But I would love to know more about who was doing what on the church premises during that time."

"You think my husband's journals would tell you that?" Mrs. Fenton asked.

"If he was as thorough in recording things as you say. At least, I would appreciate the opportunity to go through the journals from that time period."

"A lot of what he wrote about is personal, family information," Carlie noted.

He understood her hesitance. If he'd had a father who cared enough to jot down notes from every day of his life, he wasn't sure he'd want some stranger going through them. Still, these journals could hold a wealth of information that might shine light on what would surely turn out to be cold-blooded murder.

"How about this?" he suggested. "Carlie, why don't we go through the journals together? I'll let you highlight the parts that you think might be pertinent to my investigation. I'll only look at the passages that you deem relevant."

"You would trust me to do that?"

"Yeah. I would."

She seemed honestly surprised. It was going out on a limb a bit, allowing her to decide what he would see and what he would not. The truth was, she could very easily hold back anything that might make her father look bad; he realized that.

But he also trusted her. At least, he wanted to trust her. As long as he could believe she was working with him on this, he would give her that trust. If at any point he felt she was holding something back, he'd just have to go to a judge and get that court order.

"I supposed that would work," she agreed. "What do you think, Mom?"

"I think it's a very good idea. No sense wasting the detective's time with all the mundane, boring stuff your father probably wrote about."

"I thought you said a lot of it was about me?" Carlie said, half joking. "All right, Detective, we'll cooperate. You can read my father's journals, so long as they are relevant to the case."

"Fine. I look forward to discovering all your deep, dark, teenage secrets," he said, risking a bit of humor.

She simply rolled her eyes. "Those will be the pages you *don't* get to read."

"Fair enough. I'll content myself with any passages about the actions of our presumed victim and the on-going construction project at the church. Information about who was involved in that will be very helpful."

"Oh, if that's the information you need, you should probably go through the old church records," Mrs. Fenton said.

"Do you have those packed away here, too?"

She shook her head. "No, I don't think so. This is just personal items. The church continued for two years after my husband passed away, so the records remained there until it shut down."

"So where are they now?" Carlie asked.

Her mother cocked her head and seemed to think about it. "With one of the church trustees, I would guess."

"Who was that back then, Mom?"

"Let's see… During that time I think our trustees were Pete Miller, Sam Burkhart and Bev Brown. Yes, that should be right."

"Are they still in the area?"

"I think so, although Pete retired from farming so they go down to Florida for the winter now. Sam still runs the pharmacy in town, and Bev lives over in that new development behind the high school."

"So, one of them still has the church records from that time period?" TJ asked.

Mrs. Fenton shrugged. "I would suppose so. When the church shut down, there was some kind of rule that we had to hold on to records for a certain period of time."

"Then we'll just have to go pay some visits," Carlie said.

TJ corrected her. "I'll go pay some visits. What were those names again?"

Carlie gave a frustrated sigh and rolled her eyes. "Look, TJ. I've known these people all my life. They'd probably be far more willing to share anything they know or whatever documents they have with me than with you."

"I'm conducting an actual investigation, not dropping in for afternoon tea."

"They might be more willing to talk to someone who *is* dropping in for afternoon tea."

"I'm sorry, Carlie, but let's play this by the book, shall we?" he said, hoping she knew him well enough to recognize that he was serious. "I've already bent the rules enough by allowing you to help me go through the journals."

Her mother must have understood his tone. "Now, Carlie, let the poor man do his job. It's official police work, after all. We don't want to get in his way, do we?"

"No, Mom, but I just—"

"Thank you, Mrs. Fenton. If you can give me those names again, I'll be on my way. Carlie, I suppose you'll need a ride back to your car at the sheriff's office?"

She shook her head. "No, I can go with my mom. I'm sure she won't mind dropping me off."

"Oh, but I'm not going back into town," her mother said quickly. "I've got to meet the decorating committee out at the club. We're gearing up for the big tournament—lots to do. You'd better ride with the detective."

TJ tried not to feel just a little bit insulted by Carlie's look of annoyance. "Really, Mom? I'm sure the last thing Detective Douglas wants is to spend more time driving around with me."

"Actually, I have really enjoyed your company," he said, mostly just to watch her roll her eyes again, but also because it was somewhat true.

"Fine. I guess another ten minutes with you won't kill me."

He gave her an overly sweet smile and reached for the box of journals.

"Oh, here…you'll want this one, too," Mrs. Fenton said, reaching out with the book she'd been holding and dropping it into the box.

TJ thanked her for her time and scooted out of the way while Carlie scooped up a stack of agendas. It certainly was quite a collection of material. Reverend Fenton must've been very thorough, indeed. If he truly had nothing to hide, no doubt TJ would find a careful record of everything the man did during the time surrounding Ricky's disappearance.

If he did have something to hide, TJ would probably be looking for gaping holes in information. Either way, he expected to learn quite a lot from the books. He only hoped Carlie would cooperate. He would hate to make this even more uncomfortable for her than it already was.

She followed him to the car, her mother trailing behind to lock the door of the storage unit. Mrs. Fenton waved at them as Carlie deposited the agendas in the back seat of the cruiser. Carlie climbed in beside TJ while her mother drove off in her own car.

"Any chance you can jot down the names of those church trustees? I'll look them up and schedule a meeting." He pulled his notebook from his pocket and flipped to an open page.

She took the pad and pulled out a pen. "I'll give them to you, but I think you'll have better results with them if I go along with you."

"You think they know some big, dark secrets that they will only divulge to you?"

"No, but I think they'd be more comfortable if—"

"I know how to do my job, Carlie," he said sharply. "I've been told I can be quite charming, in fact."

"Like you're being right now?"

"Like I've been all along. Look, I understand this is really hard for you. I'm sorry to have to dredge up painful stuff, but there's no way around it. You know how this works—you know the law. I am bound by oath to integrity and honor. I have to look into any leads I find, and that's what I'm going to do. I'm sorry if your father's name is mixed up in it. The last thing I want to do is damage a good man's reputation."

"He really *was* a good man."

"And I believe you. So let me do my job, and we can find out who really did this thing, okay?"

"Haven't you already decided it was my father?"

He shook his head. "Of course not. But won't you and your mother feel better when I gather enough information to actually prove he wasn't involved?"

"And you expect to find that information when you look at those old church records?"

"You think I won't?"

"I think you'll find a bunch of documentation with his signature, authorizing work being done at the site there."

"And you assume that will be all I'll need to declare him guilty of disposing of a body."

"I know you're very motivated to solve this case. I just want to know that you'll get the whole picture."

He clutched the wheel, anger threatening to spill out into his conversation. "Do you distrust police in general, or is it something personal about me?"

"It's nothing personal about you at all! I'm interested in finding the truth, Detective. I hope you are, too."

"I will find the truth, Carlie. Whatever it is. If you are committed to helping me, then I'm willing to work with you. Let me hang on to the journals for now, but you can take the agendas. Look them over, then call me. We can meet up again. I'll tell you what I found about church records, and you can tell me what you found in your dad's day planners."

He could tell she was surprised that he would trust

her this far. He really had no reason to, especially since she'd practically accused him of being willing to settle for flimsy evidence against her father to achieve a quick resolution. Trusting her was risky, and he didn't like to take risks.

Maybe just this once, though, he'd consider it less of a risk and more of a leap of faith.

Chapter Nine

Carlie spent the rest of that day and all of the next in her office. It was good that she had back-to-back appointments—quite honestly, she needed the business. But those day planners she'd brought from the storage unit had been calling to her for a day and a half now.

Finally, she'd have a chance to pull yesterday's leftovers out of the mini fridge and start reading through her father's notes as she ate dinner. She knew it would be bittersweet. She didn't know, though, if it would actually shed any light on the investigation.

There were three binders, one for each of the years surrounding the time when that body had been buried. No doubt there were many, many more of these planners still in the storage unit, but this would be a good start. TJ had the bulk of what they'd retrieved. The box of journals had been full.

The books Carlie had covered one year each. They were separated into months, with tab markers designating each week of each month. Her father had put his deepest thoughts into his journals, but he'd certainly kept good notes regarding his day-to-day schedules. If he had gone to a conference during the time when Tamara received that postcard from Ricky, it would be mentioned in her dad's accounts.

Carlie pulled out that year's planner. Thumbing through, she tried not to get distracted by the memories. Certain days popped out—birthdays, special occasions, family vacations—but she didn't have time to look at those. She found August and began searching through her father's daily appointments.

As expected, he was meticulous. He even recorded the times and places he got haircuts. She found entries for counseling sessions—usually he simply used the initials of the person he would be counseling, for privacy purposes, she supposed—and entries for church board meetings. He even recorded the hour he had set aside for a weekly podcast he apparently subscribed to.

As she flipped pages into September, she saw nothing that indicated he'd been preparing to leave town. No meetings or phone calls showed up on his day-to-day calendar that seemed to say he was coordinating with church leaders to act in his absence—she clearly recalled he often spent a week or two in careful preparation before he needed to leave. Her conviction that she would find nothing at all that might connect him to that postcard increased as she scanned through the first full week of the month.

Then she came upon Saturday. The note boxes for weekend days were smaller than the weekdays, which had always seemed ironic, considering her father did so much of his work on the weekends. But on this particular Saturday, she saw no appointments or detailed schedule. All she saw on this date was one notation in blue ink that had been scribbled out in red.

She could read the letters in blue, though. They were simply "Ft Sam trip."

It was hard not to realize what that meant. Her father had planned a trip to Fort Samuel at the very time that postcard was mailed! But surely, he hadn't gone. He'd scratched the words out in his calendar. That must have meant his plans had been canceled. Unless it meant he had tried to hide it.

It couldn't be true. There was no way her father had sent that postcard. He simply wouldn't do such a thing. He would not have killed Ricky or buried his body or sent a false postcard to deceive the family. She would never believe it.

TJ, however, might. He would see this as evidence against her father. Despite what he'd said about seeking the truth, he would have little reason to keep seeking after she showed him this.

Carlie slammed the book shut. Maybe she wouldn't show him. Could she just sit on it? Withhold important evidence? It would be very wrong.

It would be just as wrong, though, to allow the whole investigation to stop just because of one vague little notation. They really had no idea what this scribble in the day planner meant. Before she showed it to TJ, she ought to at least have a clearer understanding of it. She owed her father that much.

She dropped her head in her hands and propped her elbows on her desk. All these emotions were draining her. It was only Wednesday, yet it felt as if this week had been going on forever.

Her worry session ended as she heard the front door open. The gal she'd hired to be her assistant had already gone for the day, so Carlie quickly got up and moved around her desk. She needed all the business she could get with her struggling new practice. Whatever emotional concerns she had right now needed to be bundled up onto a shelf and ignored.

She stepped out of her office into the reception area, manufacturing a bright smile for whoever might be waiting there.

Her smile faded when she saw TJ. "Oh. I thought we said I was going to call you and schedule a time to meet up."

"I thought maybe you'd be okay with meeting now."

"Um, I'm kind of busy."

He glanced around her very obviously empty office. "You don't look busy."

"I've got files to go over."

"So do I," he said. "But it's dinnertime. Have you eaten?"

"I've got leftovers in the fridge."

"Then they'll still be leftover tomorrow. Come on, my treat. I thought you might want to hear what I found out when I called that conference center in Fort Samuel."

"You called them?"

"Yes, and they were quite helpful."

"What did you find out?"

"Let's eat first. I'll tell you over dinner."

"But I…"

"Jack's Grill is right across the street. I know you like their baked sweet potatoes."

"How do you know I like the baked sweet potatoes?"

"Everybody likes the baked sweet potatoes. Come on. Please?"

It felt a bit like fraternizing with the enemy, but she was awfully hungry and she really did like Jack's sweet potatoes. "All right. Let me grab my purse."

She pulled her bag from the drawer where she had stashed it, and her glance caught on the day planner. As an agent of the law, she really ought to turn it over to TJ. He hadn't mentioned it yet, though. Maybe it would be all right to leave it here, just for now. She could always give it to him after dinner.

If he asked for it.

"Just don't go ordering the most expensive stuff on the menu," he said as she pulled the door shut behind her and locked it.

"You offer to treat, and then you give me a bunch of rules?" she said, but it was clear he'd been joking.

"I'm not some high-powered attorney. I've got to eat on a policeman's pay."

"A detective's pay," she corrected.

He laughed but accepted the correction. "And I'm a good one, at that. Wait until you hear what I dug up from the conference center."

She cringed. "Maybe you should not say 'dug up,' okay?"

TJ was still questioning his sanity. Why on earth had he asked Carlie out to dinner? He hadn't meant to. He really had just gone to her office to find out what she'd seen in her father's day planners and to let her know what he'd discovered when he'd called the conference center in Fort Samuel.

The suggestion of dinner had come out of the blue. He must've really been hungry to impulsively invite Carlie to join him rather than waiting until his visit with her was done. But Jack's Grill was right across the street, and the smell of steak and ribs filled this whole area of town. His involuntary reaction to an empty belly and the tempting aroma had to be the explanation for his impromptu invitation.

The fact that she'd accepted defied all explanation, however.

They were seated in a comfortable booth, and the server took their orders. Melfield wasn't a big town so there weren't too many restaurants to choose from, but Jack's Grill was better than it needed to be. TJ was always up for a reason to visit. Sitting across from Carlie, he realized he'd never come here with a woman.

But this wasn't a date. This was work. This was part of his investigation. He would keep that thought firmly in mind, no matter how personable Carlie could be— when she wasn't interfering with his investigation—or how bright her eyes were in the dim light of the restaurant.

He had asked about her work, if she was finding enough to keep her busy in this little town. She'd been telling him about the upswing in the need for real estate law as Melfield was going through quite a boom in housing construction these days. He'd been nodding politely.

"But enough about that," she said. "Tell me what you found out from Fort Samuel."

He took a quick sip of his water and readjusted his focus. He'd been noticing how one stray wisp of her hair was curled gracefully along the contour of her neck. It was very important that he not notice things like that—especially with Carlie.

"You might be gratified to know that they actually remember your father there," he said.

Her obvious surprise turned into a cautious smile. "They do? How is that?"

"For good reasons, I assure you. I spoke with the manager there, and she recalls many of the events your father was involved with. Apparently, he was on the planning committee for the ecumenical body that sponsored a lot of these conferences and retreats. He left a very favorable impression with the people who work there. In fact, the manager specifically asked that I extend her sympathies to you. So, here I am, extending them. The Eastwood Conference and Retreat Center is very sorry for your loss."

"Well, thank you. That's very sweet. They really remember him?"

"Absolutely."

Now Carlie's smile faded. "So...she remembered the times my father was there. Was he...did she know the actual dates of those events he attended?"

"It was all in their records. She looked it up for me, and I'm happy to tell you, there was no indication he was involved in any event during August or September of the year that postcard was sent."

"So he wasn't there? You're sure of it?"

"Of course. Aren't you?" He had to laugh at her sudden lack of confidence. "I thought you said there was no way he'd been involved in sending the postcard."

"He wasn't... Naturally, I'm positive that he wasn't.

I just didn't think you'd be so easy to convince. Are you convinced?"

"I am. Unless you found something in those day planners? Was there any mention in them of a conference he was involved in?"

"What? No, no mention of any conference at all."

"Then it would seem to me that I'll need to keep hunting for my guilty party."

Her smile was huge and brilliant this time. "Yes! Yes, it does look like that, doesn't it? Oh, look, our food is here. I didn't even realize how hungry I am."

Their meals had indeed arrived, and TJ's stomach growled loudly in response. Carlie laughed. He probably should've been embarrassed, but she seemed so amused by it that he simply laughed along with her.

They dug in and conversation focused on their food for a bit. The meat was cooked perfectly, the broccoli with almonds had just enough garlic, and the baked sweet potatoes did not disappoint. Finally, TJ remembered this was supposed to be a work meeting, so he brought the discussion back to matters at hand.

"I found those church records I wanted to look at, too."

"Oh? You mean regarding the digging at the foundation that went on twelve years ago?"

"Yes. I contacted the church trustees your mother mentioned and found out Mrs. Beverly Brown is the current keeper of the records."

"Well, she still lives here in town. That's great."

"Yes and no. She's the keeper of the keys for the file cabinet they're stored in, but she doesn't actually have the records."

"Then where are they?"

"At my brother's church."

"Faith Community? Why on earth are they there?"

"It makes sense, actually. Since most of the congregation migrated there when Epiphany closed, it seemed logical to keep their records there. This way anyone who needs access to baptismal records or whatever knows where to find them."

"So you've gone over to look at them?"

"No, the file cabinets are locked and Mrs. Brown has the keys."

"Won't she open them for you?"

"As soon as she's back in town. Apparently, she's off visiting family for a while."

"Oh no! When will she return?"

"Saturday night. She promises to be in church Sunday morning, and I told her I'd meet her then to look at the files."

"That's only a few days away. What do you think you'll find?"

"Names, dates, contracts... I'm hoping to learn who had access to that site and what their work orders told them to do there."

"You mean you want to find out if my dad had anything to do with ending the job and filling in that hole before the foundation was actually fixed."

"I want to find out anything I can. Trust me, Carlie. I'm not trying to pin this on your father. I'm looking for the truth."

"And you think the truth is in those files?"

"Some of it is, no doubt. We just have to find out how much they will tell us."

"*We?*"

"Yes, *we*. If you'll be at church on Sunday, why don't you meet Mrs. Brown with me? You know her better than I do, right?"

"I guess I can be at church on Sunday. All right, if you're willing to let me look at those records with you, I suppose I can—"

He could tell she was trying to hide her appreciation for being asked to help. But now she was interrupted as a passing restaurant patron noticed her.

"Carlie! Oh, my, look at you, dining with the enemy."

TJ wasn't sure he appreciated that particular phrase. He'd been specifically working to convince Carlie he was *not* the enemy. Had she been talking so badly about him to her friends?

"Margie, how nice to see you," Carlie greeted, giving a cool but polite smile.

"Is your mother with you tonight?" The woman went on, not waiting for Carlie to answer. "I can't imagine how hard all this must be for her, and for you, of course. What a shock it must be. Such a tragedy for your poor family."

"And for the LeMaster family," Carlie said, pointing out what she clearly thought should be the woman's bigger concern.

This Margie woman hardly missed a beat. She leaned in toward their table and her voice dropped just a bit lower but lost none of its melodrama. "It's such a shame everything has to come out now. We had such fond memories of your father, too. But I suppose the paper is right. We can't be too hasty to place blame, even though the evidence is…well, you know."

Carlie shot TJ a questioning glance. He gave her a confused shrug and shook his head. He assumed Margie was referencing the tragedy of finding a body two days ago, but beyond that he had no idea what the woman was talking about.

"What do you mean?" Carlie asked her. "What paper?"

"The *Melfield Mid-Day*," Margie replied. "You must have seen the article on the front page today."

Carlie gave TJ another glance. This one came with an angry glare. All he could do was offer a more enthusiastic shrug. He recognized the name of the local newspaper, of course, but wasn't aware of any article in it.

"No, I haven't seen the paper today," Carlie said, still glaring at TJ.

"Oh, well, here." Margie dug into her oversize handbag and, with a flourish, slapped a newspaper in front of Carlie. "I can get another copy. Go ahead and take mine."

"No, really that's not—" Carlie stopped protesting and pulled the newspaper up to read the headline. "Oh no!"

"I'm so sorry, dear," Margie said with delighted pity. "None of us would have ever suspected, I'm sure. Such a tragedy for everyone!" She shook her head with affected sadness and *tsk-tsked*.

TJ craned his neck to try to see the paper, but Carlie monopolized it. He couldn't enjoy the relief of no longer being subjected to her angry glare, because when he glanced up, he noticed Margie had taken over that task.

Her voice was full of disdain when she spoke. "I hope you haven't been interrogating the poor girl over her dinner."

"No, we were—" He caught himself.

Whoever this woman was, he did not owe her any kind of explanation. He did, however, wish he could do something about the look of despair that was sweeping over Carlie's face.

"What does it say?" he asked.

Carlie turned the paper around so he could see it. The headline jumped out boldly. It read "Body Found at Local Church, Minister Suspected."

He met Carlie's desperate gaze and could see the shock she felt at reading those words. Her eyes displayed a whole range of emotion—pain, disbelief, frustration and anger. Slowly, her expression changed and her eyes narrowed.

He recognized a new emotion on her face. It was one he knew well, and it cut right through him. He knew exactly what she felt—her flashing eyes practically screamed the accusation.

Betrayal.

Chapter Ten

How dare TJ give this interview to the newspaper! Naturally, the article was vague, crediting "a source at the sheriff's office closely involved in the investigation," but who was closer to the investigation than TJ?

It was unthinkable he could carry on casual conversation with her when he'd just told some local reporter that her father was guilty of murder. Sure, maybe he still used words like *alleged* and *suspect*, but no one reading the paper would notice that. Everyone in town would see the headline and think only one thing: Reverend Fenton had murdered Ricky LeMaster.

And they still didn't even have a positive ID on the poor kid. That wouldn't slow the gossip, though. Everyone knew the body was most likely Ricky's, and this article connected her father to it.

She was too furious for words. Furious and—if she was honest with herself—hurt. Grabbing her purse, she scooted out of the booth and pushed past Margie. So what if she appeared rude? Nothing mattered now. Her father was practically convicted, and there was nothing she could do about it.

She should have trusted her instinct about TJ in the first place. He was merely another ambitious detective eager to pin this crime on an easy target so he could take credit. He wasn't looking for facts, just another pat on the back.

He called after her, but she ignored him. What a fool she was. She'd actually been enjoying the evening. She'd even thought maybe she could believe him when he talked about truth! How had she misjudged him so thoroughly?

Well, one thing she knew for sure. She'd made the right decision not to show him that entry in her dad's day planner. Wouldn't that be just what he needed to close the book on this case! What did it matter if some receptionist at the conference center didn't recall him being there that week? Carlie had a calendar entry in his own handwriting.

TJ might think he had more than enough circumstantial evidence so far, but the last thing she wanted was for him to get his hands on more. Would he still demand to see the day planner now that he'd talked to the woman at the conference center? Maybe not. Maybe he'd just take her word for it that there was nothing incriminating. Maybe now was the perfect time to head back to her office and get that day planner locked up somewhere and safely forgotten.

She left TJ behind and stormed out of the restaurant.

Waiting on traffic, she kept glancing over her shoulder, expecting him to come rushing out of Jack's Grill after her. He didn't, though. She darted across the street, fumbling in her purse to find her keys. If she could just get inside her office and lock the door behind her, she wouldn't have to see him again.

She had the key in the lock and was jostling the doorknob when she heard him call her name from across the street. Was it worth it to turn around and reply? No. She jiggled the knob and grumbled when it refused to open. Why hadn't she spent the money to replace it two weeks ago when it first started giving her trouble?

"Carlie!" he called again.

This time, she did turn. It was too late to avoid him. With a sigh, she waited for him to jog across the street and come up her walkway. His hair still needed a trim, even more evident now after his hurried run. She made herself stop staring at the errant curls.

"Look, I don't know anything about that article in the paper," he said, slightly winded.

"The reporter didn't tell you when they'd be running it?"

"What reporter? I didn't talk to anyone, and I certainly didn't authorize anyone else to do it. What did the article say?"

"It said exactly what you've been thinking all along, that Ricky was murdered and my father is the prime suspect. Now the whole town thinks that's the truth!"

"How do you know what I've been thinking? I've never said anyone is my prime suspect. I'm conducting an investigation—that means everyone with any connection to this case is a person of interest."

"Well, who gave all this information to the newspaper then?"

"All *what* information? I still haven't seen today's newspaper."

"Here!" she shoved it at him and finally managed to unlock her office.

He followed her in. "It simply says we're investigating."

"It says you already have a suspect! And it says my father is the last person to see Ricky alive. I wonder who told them that."

She tossed her purse into one of the chairs near the reception desk and turned on him. He was busy scanning the article, a scowl creasing his brow.

"I certainly didn't tell anyone that," he said gruffly. "I wasn't even aware of it myself. Is it true? Was your father the last person to see Ricky alive?"

"Of course not!"

"So why did they include that in this article?"

"Apparently, it came from some mysterious source at the sheriff's office. I assumed, since you're head detective, you'd know about it."

"Well, I don't. Maybe you should stop assuming things about me."

"So the reporter just made this up?"

"He must have."

"I don't believe that. He wouldn't print it if someone hadn't told him, and he indicates the person he spoke to is a part of the investigation. Since you're head of the department, what else can I think?"

"Really? You're going to believe this mysterious source over me when I stand right here and tell you to your face that I have no reason to believe your father murdered Ricky LeMaster?"

"You don't?"

"Of course not. There's not a shred of real evidence to tie him to it."

"So why have you been investigating him?"

"I'm not investigating *him*, I'm investigating the *case*! I thought you'd be relieved when I told you what I'd learned from the conference center and when I invited you to join me on Sunday to go over the old church records. Doesn't that tell you I'm not out to get your father?"

"It tells me maybe you don't trust me and want to keep an eye on me or something."

He rolled his eyes. "You are so much like a lawyer."

"I *am* a lawyer."

"I don't know why I thought I could work with you. I should've known better."

"And what's that supposed to mean? All lawyers are impossible to work with?"

She expected him to deny that was what he'd meant. He didn't, though, and he could probably read the surprise on her face.

"Yeah. They are," he said simply.

"Wow. You don't think that's a bit…unfair?"

"In my experience, no. Lawyers exist only to get in the way of the law—they twist it and manipulate it to serve their purpose."

"That's not what we do."

"It's what I've seen. Admit it—you've seen it, too. The big high-paying clients go free while innocent victims get left behind. Isn't that what they taught you at Blakely & Burke?"

"I left Blakely & Burke."

"Yeah. I guess you did, but not before…"

"Not before what?"

"Look, I didn't come over here to dig into my ancient history. I came to remind you that if you really do want to help with this case, if you truly want to get to the truth, you need to trust me."

"What about the newspaper?"

"There's nothing we can do about it," he said. "People are going to talk, you know that. I didn't give any interview, but maybe someone did. Maybe it was someone just wanting attention, maybe someone with something to hide. The only way to know is to keep searching for answers. That's what I'm going to do. Are you in for that or not?"

She knew he was right. She'd accused him of jumping to conclusions about her father, and now she had done the same thing about him. She claimed she wanted truth… Now was the time to decide if she really meant that. Could she want it enough to trust him?

Could she trust her father enough to show TJ that day planner?

Somehow it felt wrong. How could she betray her father that way? Then again, how could she say she wanted truth if she persisted in keeping secrets?

She *did* want the truth, no matter what it was. If she honestly believed her father was innocent, it was an insult to his legacy to withhold evidence. She had to do the right thing and trust TJ to continue seeking the truth.

"I think you should see something," she said, swallowing back her hesitation.

TJ studied the words in the day planner. They were partially crossed out but still easily legible. Obviously, if someone had been trying to hide something, they would've done a much better job of obliterating the note. From all appearances, the entry was simply crossed out as a cancellation rather than to deceive.

But the meaning was painfully clear: "Ft Sam trip." It appeared that Carlie's father had at least planned a trip to Fort Samuel on the first Saturday of September, eleven years ago. That would have been right around the time Tamara Scheuster received the postcard, based on what she'd said about it arriving shortly before her wedding. TJ had looked up the man's profile to be sure of his anniversary date. There was no doubt; the reverend's notation was smack-dab in the middle of the window of opportunity.

Carlie's father *could* have been the one to mail the postcard. But why would he have sent it from Fort Samuel when there was no other reason for him to be there? That seemed suspicious. And would he really have written the town name in his planner, only to carelessly cross the words out? If the man had been actively involved in covering up a murder, he certainly hadn't been going about his deception very well. Why not erase the note or completely blot it out? Why even write it down in the first place?

The very fact that the notation was there, only lightly scratched off, told TJ that Reverend Fenton had not been trying to hide anything at all. Every instinct told him that such a detail-oriented man would have been much more careful if he had been covering for a murder. Still, TJ couldn't ignore the words on that page.

"Do you remember this?" he asked Carlie.

"I was a senior in high school and busy with all those

teenage things. I really can't remember what my father was doing."

"So you don't know if he went to Fort Samuel that weekend."

"No, but why else would he write it in his day planner?"

"He crossed it out."

"You don't think he went?"

"I have no reason to believe that he did."

"Really?"

"You think I'm wrong? He *did* go to Fort Samuel that weekend? But you've been insisting he had nothing to do with any of it."

"He didn't!" she exclaimed, her frustration evident.

"Then why are you so worried about this one little entry in his day planner?"

"Because you might think it makes him look guilty!"

"But I *don't* think it makes him look guilty!"

She paused. "You really don't?"

"No."

"You have another suspect?"

"Not yet, but so far, I've not found proof that your father did anything to anyone," TJ said. Before he let her get too comfortable, he quickly went on. "That's not to say he isn't a primary person of interest. I'm absolutely going to go over those journals with a fine-tooth comb."

"You haven't looked at them yet?"

"I was waiting for you. I know your father wrote about personal matters and family things. I don't need to know all the Fenton family secrets, just those relevant to our case."

She nodded and seemed to contemplate his words. "All right, then. When do you want to work on that?"

"Tomorrow. Do you have some free time?"

"I've got meetings in the morning, but my afternoon is free."

He pulled out his phone and checked his own schedule. "That looks good for me, too. Can we say one o'clock at my office?"

"Perfect. I'll see you then."

He quickly added it to his schedule. There was no way to be sure they'd find anything useful, but he was glad to know he could trust Carlie. It must've been difficult for her to show him that day planner entry. She hadn't brought it up over dinner, but in the end, she'd done the right thing.

He hated to realize how unexpected that was. Perhaps she'd been correct about him—he was being unfair in his assumptions about her. She wasn't just another lawyer out to sway a jury or win a judgment through manipulations and legal juggling. Even when she feared it would cast guilt on her own father, she'd turned over the evidence.

She put truth ahead of her own agenda. TJ had seen painfully little of that during his career. He really had been wrong about her.

Unsure of what else to say, and not really comfortable with his own sudden awareness of just how easy it was becoming to trust her, TJ slid his phone back into his pocket and cleared his throat.

"Great. Tomorrow at one."

"Tomorrow at one," she repeated. "Should I bring along the day planners?"

"Might as well. We can cross-reference to keep dates and events straight."

"And we can get an idea of the time surrounding that digging project at the church," she suggested. "That should help us know what to look for when we're going through the records at your brother's church on Sunday."

"True. Good plan, Carlie."

She smiled an honest, grateful smile. "Thanks."

TJ cleared his throat again. What was wrong with him? He couldn't form a single word. Instead, he just returned her smile, pushed his hair back and made some excuse about needing to hurry back to his office.

She seemed relieved to see him go, so he went. Out on the front stoop of the little storefront that had been converted to office space, he heard her lock the door behind him. It was a simple, ordinary act, but it reminded TJ that there was a barrier between them. She held fast to her father's innocence, even when it seemed there might be reason to doubt. TJ, however, had learned to doubt everyone.

Heading back to where he'd parked his car, he realized they seemed to have a couple things in common. Aside from choosing professions that centered on law, they both valued truth, they both had lost people they loved, and—it seemed—they both had grown up in church, with a strong faith.

He wondered if Carlie had managed to hold on to hers. He knew only too well that his own had slipped away. What would the preacher's daughter think of him if she knew about that?

Carlie waited until she saw TJ get into his car and drive away before she shut off the lights at her office and left it again. Why was she avoiding him? She'd just made an appointment to meet him tomorrow. Was she afraid of him or something?

No, she didn't feel anything like fear toward TJ. Did she trust him? Perhaps. He'd certainly surprised her tonight, being so charming over dinner. For a while there, it had felt almost like, well, almost like she was with a friend. That had been very unexpected.

Hoisting her purse over her shoulder and clutching her laptop case, Carlie headed up the street toward her apartment. Melfield wasn't a big place, but the downtown area was still bustling even on a Wednesday night. The streetlights were on although the June sun hadn't quite set. Cars waited at the light in the center of town and Carlie hurried through the crosswalk. Her apartment was on the second story, above a shoe repair shop and a jeweler.

She wondered where TJ lived. Maybe in that new development on the other side of town? There were some nice apartments there, with a clubhouse and a pool. Or maybe he owned a house in one of the neighborhoods. Did he have a dog? Once she got herself settled here in Melfield again, she was definitely getting a dog.

She really didn't know very much about TJ. She hadn't thought a lot about him. But now…she'd seen a side to him that caught her attention. Not that she was interested in him. No, that was the last thing on her mind. He was just…

He was interesting. In a professional way. That's all it was.

Unlocking her front door, she gathered up the mail that had come through the postal slot today. Her landing consisted of little more than an area to keep a coat stand and a welcome mat, so she pulled the door shut and plodded up the long flight of stairs to get to her living area. Some days, the climb felt longer than others, and today was one of those days.

Dropping her things onto the bench near the entry, she kicked off her shoes and made a beeline for the kitchen for a tall glass of iced tea. She probably shouldn't have stormed out of the restaurant the way she had. No doubt people had noticed and thought the worst. Someone would probably even call her mother to mention it.

Of course, she needed to call her mom tonight. There was no doubt she'd see that awful newspaper article. As hard as it had hit Carlie, it would be even worse for her mom. To see those horrible things in print! She'd be upset, for sure.

Carlie retrieved her phone from her purse and plopped down in an armchair. She didn't tap in her mom's number right away, though. She needed a minute. Her own emotions were tangled and frayed—how could she hope to provide any comfort to her mom?

She jumped when the phone vibrated in her hand.

It was her mother. Naturally. She must have just seen the paper. Carlie took another big swig of iced tea and answered.

"You were out on a date with Detective TJ?" her mother's voice practically shouted.

"What? No! What are you talking about, Mom?"

"Margie Sanders said she saw you at Jack's with him just a little while ago."

Carlie grimaced. It hadn't even dawned on her

what people might think—what her own mother might think—about her and TJ getting dinner together.

"We had some stuff to go over, Mom, and it was dinnertime. It was absolutely *not* a date."

"Margie said it sure looked like a date. He paid for your meal, didn't he?"

"Yes, but only because I... Look, Mom. Did Margie tell you what we were talking about there?"

"She said you looked pretty cozy until someone showed you that dumb newspaper article."

"Cozy until...? Margie showed me that article! And we were not cozy. But, Mom, did you see the paper?"

"I did, yes. I'll tell that editor just what I think about that kind of reporting, too! Honestly, as if anyone will believe that garbage."

"So you aren't worried about it?"

"Of course not. Why should I? It's not like the police have any real evidence against your father. How could they? He didn't do anything, so there is no proof."

"But they quoted someone from the sheriff's office saying he's a prime suspect."

"Oh, honey. Don't let that upset you. Some newspapers will print anything. Besides, your detective is trying to find the real killer, isn't he?"

"Well, yes, but...he's not my detective. You can't go around saying things like that, Mom."

"All right, I understand. Whatever is going on, you've got to keep up professional appearances and all that."

"Mom! There's nothing going on."

"When are you seeing him again?"

"Tomorrow, but it's not like that. We're meeting at his office to go through Dad's journals."

"Oh. He really is letting you look at them, too?"

"He's being very generous, Mom. Besides, he doesn't have time to comb through all the unrelated stuff in there—you know how much Dad wrote. I can help screen it for him."

"I'm glad you two are getting along so well. Maybe this weekend you can take a break from investigating and do something fun."

"We have more investigating to do on the weekend, actually. We're already scheduled to meet Bev Brown after church on Sunday to go over some of the old records from Epiphany. TJ thinks we can learn something about who was in charge of the work being done on the foundations at the time."

Her mom was quiet for a moment. "Bev still has all those old records?"

"Yes, the trustees kept everything after the church decided to close. It's all locked up in a file cabinet at Faith Community Church."

"All of it? There must've been years and years of records."

"It must be a big file cabinet. All I know is Bev has the key and she won't be back until Saturday night, so we're meeting her on Sunday."

"To find out who was in charge of all that digging back then."

"Something like that. So…you'll be in church on Sunday, Mom?"

"Of course, honey."

"Maybe I'll go, too. I mean, since I have to be there right after the service, I should probably attend."

"That's wonderful! I know you've still got some

mixed feelings about everyone leaving Epiphany and going over to Faith Community, but you know it's the same Lord, no matter which sanctuary you sit in."

"I know, Mom."

"And you'll love the new song our choir has. We've been working on it more than a month. I can't wait for you to hear it."

"I know it'll be beautiful. But...you're sure you're not too upset by that article in the newspaper today?"

"Oh, honey, of course I'm upset by it. But you can't let that trouble you. Just because the newspaper prints some lies about your father doesn't make them the truth. We both know he would never try to cause harm to someone, right? That's what's important—we need to remember him for the good man that he was."

"You're right," Carlie conceded.

"I'm just glad you've made friends with that nice young detective. He's really good-looking, don't you think?"

"Stop it, Mom."

"Well, he is, isn't he?"

"I'm hanging up now."

"Don't tell me you can't even recognize when a man is nice-looking!"

"Goodbye, Mom."

"Fine. Have a good night, honey. We can both rest well, knowing there's a good man working on this terrible case."

Carlie ended the call, somewhat relieved her mother was being sensible about the newspaper article. Too bad she wasn't so sensible about Detective TJ. Her mom had called him nice-looking! It's true he was, but Carlie hardly needed her mother pointing it out every five minutes.

She finished off her glass of tea and stretched her weary muscles, trying to relieve the tension that had built up in her neck and shoulders. At least she didn't have to go to sleep tonight with the burden of hiding that entry she'd found in her father's day planner. No matter how much she didn't know about TJ, she trusted him to do the right thing.

She shouldn't have assumed the worst about him. She shouldn't have run out on dinner the way she had, either. And she shouldn't have just ignored it when he'd referred to his own "ancient history" during their conversation about her work with Blakely & Burke. What did her old law firm in Louisville have to do with his personal past?

Indeed, there were so many things she didn't know about TJ. She was glad they'd be meeting up again tomorrow. It might give her a chance to start learning.

Chapter Eleven

TJ had spent the morning catching up on his files and making phone calls. He'd reminded the coroner they were all still waiting for a positive identification and was assured one would be issued as soon as possible. He'd checked the clock frequently, unwilling to admit to himself how eager he was for one o'clock to arrive.

Finally, he had his work mostly done and realized there would be just enough time to heat up some leftovers for a quick lunch before his scheduled meeting with Carlie. He didn't get a chance, though. Sheriff Villa surprised him by knocking at the door frame of TJ's office.

"Got a minute, TJ?"

"Sure, come on in."

"Just thought I'd check on how things are going on the LeMaster case."

"Well, so far, I can't say it actually is the LeMaster case, but our coroner promises to get us positive ID very soon."

"It's the LeMaster kid," the sheriff said, shaking his

Susan Gee Heino 129

head. "Too bad. We all sort of hoped he was still out there somewhere."

"Yeah. Any word how Scheuster and his family are doing?"

"He's still taking some days off, staying at the in-laws while everyone comes to terms with this, I guess."

"That's the best thing. I talked to him and his wife briefly the day the body was found. She seemed pretty broken up."

"All the more reason we need to get some answers for them. You did good, getting started right away with that minister. Seems everything points in his direction, huh?"

"Reverend Fenton? No, I wouldn't say that."

"Seems like you could. I read your reports—and that stuff in the newspaper. Who told you the reverend was the last person to see Ricky?"

"No one told me that. I don't know how it got into the newspaper," TJ assured him. "There's nothing concrete tying him to this at all."

"Maybe not concrete, but you got all that talk of him fighting with the kid. I'm sure the Fenton girl told you she broke up with him, and he didn't take it very well. Seems the boy made some pretty nasty threats that would get any father riled up for his daughter."

"They had words, but there was no violence involved," TJ said.

"Well, there was violence involved at some point, right there at the church. The kid was buried in a hole that the reverend himself was in charge of digging. And filling in, it seems."

"I'm still looking into that aspect."

"Don't take too long. The whole town has a real interest in this case. They're going to expect our new big-city head detective to solve it lickety-split."

"I'm doing my best, sir."

"I know you are. I'm just saying…this case has gotten pretty cold over the last dozen years. We all know how seldom a crime this old gets solved. When you've got a suspect with so much circumstantial evidence, it might pay to not waste so much time looking elsewhere. Especially if, you know, that suspect isn't exactly here to require a long, expensive trial."

TJ had a hard time believing he'd heard the man right. Shelby Villa was a bit rough around the edges, sure, but TJ had never doubted he was a straight arrow. He'd been a deputy for several years but was elected sheriff four years ago. He seemed loved and respected by everyone. Could he honestly be asking TJ to shortchange his investigation just for the sake of public relations?

Well, maybe that was how Sheriff Villa thought he could win reelection, but TJ was not about to compromise like that. Not even if he thought there was a chance Reverend Fenton had actually been involved. No, he would not call any case solved unless he knew for a fact that it was.

"I'm sorry, sir, but I can't work that way," he said sharply. "I'm not ignoring any facts in my investigation, but I'm certainly not going to pretend any of them mean something they don't. Right now, I don't know who killed that boy twelve years ago. Until I have something real, some sound evidence that would stand up to a jury, I'm not going to point my finger at anyone. If you want to handle things differently, then you'll need a different head detective."

He had a moment of panic when he was afraid Villa might just take him up on that offer and tell him to gather his things. But the older man simply chuckled and shook his head.

"All right, Douglas. You're just bullheaded enough to figure this one out, I guess. But don't get so distracted by Miss Fenton that you don't see real blame if it's there."

"I'm not getting distracted by anyone, sir. I'm just doing my job the way it's supposed to be done. Miss Fenton trusts me with that. I hope you do, too."

The sheriff laughed and just shook his head again. "I trust you, son. Just be careful. The public needs someone to get mad at over this horrible thing. They want the truth, too, but they won't wait forever to get it. If you can't give them the right murderer, then they might just decide on one for themselves. All your hard work to protect the good reverend might end up wasted when the court of public opinion weighs in. Don't let Miss Fenton's pretty face slow you down, okay?"

"Miss Fenton's pretty face is just as eager to find the truth as I am, sir."

He felt somewhat ridiculous even saying the words, but the sheriff seemed to find them amusing. He was still chuckling as he told TJ to have a good afternoon and went on his way. Apparently, the man wasn't offended by TJ's reaction to his questionable advice. Would the sheriff really accept a report from TJ filled with sketchy detail and circumstantial evidence as good enough reason to close the case?

He truly hoped not. He'd thought when he came to work here that he'd see less politics and shady dealing. The sheriff's words left him feeling more than a little disappointed.

It didn't matter, though. He knew all about public opinion and how fickle it could be. The good people of Melfield might talk fondly of their former pastor, but he'd already seen how quickly one little newspaper article could make them doubt the man. TJ would not let that—or any of the very pleasant things about Carlie— slow him down.

They were in a race to clear Reverend Fenton's name and they both knew it. This time he would not fail. The truth *would* come out before another innocent person suffered.

Carlie waited, her back pressed against the cold hallway wall just around the corner from TJ's office. The security officer on duty had let her in.

As she'd come up to TJ's office, she'd heard voices and caught a glimpse of the sheriff standing in the doorway. She'd paused, not sure if she should interrupt, then realized they were talking about the case. The sheriff had seemed to be urging TJ to solve the case quickly, to consider any evidence he might have against her father as more than enough to determine his guilt. She'd been shocked and was just about to charge in and tell the man what she thought about that idea, but TJ's response had stopped her. He'd stood up to his superior; he even indicated he would leave his job before he'd throw Carlie's dad under the bus.

Then she'd heard her own name mentioned. Was

the sheriff concerned she was getting too close to TJ? That was the last thing she wanted. If anyone thought that…well, it could certainly prevent her from being involved in the rest of this investigation. But did she dare step aside now? It was a surprise to hear TJ stick up for her father, but could she really trust him to investigate fairly? Should she confront him or just walk away?

She was still trying to decide what to do when she heard the sheriff laugh and make some quick small talk before leaving TJ's office. Carlie was ashamed at herself for eavesdropping; being discovered here would be mortifying. She slunk back, ducking around a corner to catch her breath and think up some logical excuse for loitering. Thankfully, the man's laughter and footsteps trailed off in the other direction. Soon the sheriff was gone. Carlie could wait just a few seconds, then show up in TJ's office as scheduled.

He wouldn't have to know how her cheeks had suddenly flamed hot when she heard him defend her and then even compliment her. Well, if she didn't want him to realize she'd overheard, she'd better wait more than a few seconds. It would take a minute or two to recover her composure.

Taking a couple deep, slow breaths she calmed herself. Thankfully, the office was practically empty right now. TJ's coworkers must be out at lunch or something.

When she was sure her coloring was normal again, and her breathing was natural, she pulled her purse back up onto her shoulder and readjusted the pile of day planners she had brought along with her. She would march up to TJ's office doorway and knock. She rounded the

corner to make a cool, calm and completely professional arrival.

Unfortunately, TJ had arrived at the corner, too. She
plowed into him. Something cold and wet hit her chest.

"Carlie!" TJ cried, steadying himself.

A plastic bowl half full of cold spaghetti dropped to
the floor. The other half of the spaghetti was plastered
to the front of Carlie's summery blue blouse. A blouse
she was probably never going to wear again.

Stunned, she just stood there watching pasta and to-
mato sauce drip off her and onto TJ's shoes. Fortunately,
in her startled surprise, she'd tossed the day planners out
of harm's way. They were scattered several feet away.

"I'm so sorry," TJ said, jumping back and rushing to
a nearby kitchenette for paper towels. "That was going
to be my lunch. The microwave is right over there."

"I don't think you're going to want to eat it now,"
she said.

He handed her a wad of paper towels and began wiping what he could off the floor. The spaghetti was a total
loss. Just like Carlie's shirt.

"No, looks like I'll be skipping lunch today. I am
so, so sorry, Carlie. Let me know what it costs to clean
your clothes—I'll pay for it."

"On a policeman's salary? That's asking an awful
lot."

He glanced up from wiping, and she was caught off
guard by the amount of concern she read in his eyes.
She smiled to let him know she wasn't angry with him.
In fact, as the cold dampness from the spaghetti sauce
began seeping through her clothes and another blob
of noodles fell onto the floor he had just wiped, she

couldn't help but laugh. So much for her plans to be professional.

"I shouldn't laugh," she said, not being able to keep from doing so. "Sorry about your lunch. It smells good, at least."

"I'm pretty good with a box of pasta and a jar of marinara sauce."

"You solve crime *and* you cook? Impressive," she said, brushing off the last of the big chunks and stooping to retrieve her father's day planners. "Look, I'm a wreck and you're probably hungry. If it's leftovers you want, I've got half a tray of lasagna my mom made. I obviously need to change clothes, so why don't you bring the journals we need to go through and come over to my apartment? We can eat while we work."

He paused for a moment to consider. She pulled at her sagging shirt, emphasizing the mess and discomfort. There was no way he could expect her to get any work done here, with spaghetti sauce plastered all over her front.

"All right," he agreed. "Let me just go grab those journals, and—"

He was interrupted by rapidly approaching footsteps from the hallway Carlie had just come through. A moment later, Tamara Scheuster appeared. She stopped in her tracks, taken aback by the two of them and the not-quite-cleaned-up spaghetti disaster.

"Um, I was hoping to talk to you, TJ," she said slowly. "But if this is a bad time…"

"No, not a bad time for talking," he replied. "Just a bad time to eat lunch. How are you, Mrs. Scheuster?"

Carlie recognized the woman's nervousness. Tamara's gaze scanned the area, anxiously on the look-out for something…or someone. Her husband, probably. But what made her appear so worried, so uneasy?

Whatever it was, Carlie realized her own presence might add to the problem. She pushed her curiosity aside and made an excuse.

"I should probably go and change my shirt."

"Please, wait," Tamara said. "I will only take a min-ute, Carlie, and you really should know about this. It's kind of important."

"Okay."

"Would you like to step into my office?" TJ asked.

Tamara glanced around the area again and nodded. She practically scurried into his open doorway like a frightened rabbit. Carlie shook off what was left of the pasta bits and let TJ usher her in behind Tamara. The rest of the mess on the floor would have to wait, she supposed. Whatever brought Ricky's sister over here today seemed to take precedence over spilled spaghetti.

"Here," she said, pulling something out of her purse. "I found that postcard."

"You found it? The postcard from your brother?" TJ asked.

"It says it's from my brother," Tamara muttered. "I thought it was…at first."

"But now you don't think so," TJ surmised.

"No. Not after I got the next one," Tamara said.

"The *next* one? You mean Ricky sent more than one postcard?" Carlie asked.

Tamara shook her head and glanced out the door-way, still nervous. "No. He didn't. I don't think he sent any of them."

"How many postcards did you get, Mrs. Scheuster?" TJ questioned.

"I got three of them. This first one came more than a year after Ricky disappeared. Like I told you, I remember exactly when it arrived. I graduated in May, and Dave and I got engaged. We set the wedding for September, but as the day got closer I started feeling like… Well, I really wasn't sure I wanted to go through with it."

"Were you and Detective Scheuster having some troubles?" TJ asked.

"No, not more than just the stuff you go through when you're too young and too much in love," she said with a sad smile. "But I just hated that Ricky wasn't there. He was my big brother and he always looked out for me. Honestly, I didn't even really know if he was happy that I was with Dave. They didn't always get along, you know."

"I thought they were best friends," Carlie said.

"They were," Tamara said. "But sometimes, friends don't agree on things. I was one of those things they didn't agree on."

"So you worried you didn't have his blessing. Is that it?" TJ asked.

"Yeah. I got kind of upset toward the end of August, all the planning and pressure and things. I was thinking about calling it off or postponing. I told everyone I didn't want to get married without Ricky there."

"But you did get married," Carlie pointed out.

"I did. That's why I remember getting the postcard so vividly. Right when I needed my brother most, this postcard showed up in the mail."

She handed it over to TJ. Carlie craned her neck to see it. She may have gotten some spaghetti sauce on TJ's sleeve in the process.

Tams—I hear your marrying Dave. If you gotta pick one, he's the best. Wish I could be there, but its safer if I stay away for a while. Love you always!—Ricky

Despite a few grammar errors, the wording of the postcard really struck Carlie.

"*Safer*? What was he running from?" she asked.

"I don't know," Tamara said. "At the time, I wanted so badly to hear from him that I really believed he sent this. We figured there were lots of things he could have meant—he'd been in trouble at school, trouble for some vandalism he'd done and he'd been fighting with someone. It could have been any of those things."

"Who was he fighting with?" TJ asked.

"Not my father," Carlie interjected. "They had an argument, but it wasn't a fight, and Ricky wasn't in any danger. Not from him."

"No, that wasn't it," Tamara agreed. "Your dad was trying to help him. He was fighting with someone else."

"Who?" Carlie and TJ both asked at the same time.

"With Mitchell Brown."

"I thought he was Ricky's other best buddy," TJ said.

"He was, but he was also my ex-boyfriend. I was kind of dating Mitch when Dave and I started going out, too. That started a fight between all three of them. Mitch and Dave were both mad at Ricky for not taking their side, and Ricky was mad at both of them *and* at me. It made him pretty difficult to be around for a while. He got kind of crazy."

Carlie shook her head in disbelief. "I had no idea about any of that. I thought he was just upset with me for breaking up with him."

"That was the icing on the cake for him. That's when he started getting into trouble, breaking things and making those wild threats," Tamara said. "None of us knew what to do. When he disappeared, I guess we thought he'd just run off to cool down for a while. We always expected him to come back."

"But all you got was a postcard," TJ said. "Is it in Ricky's handwriting?"

"I thought so," Tamara said. "At first. But when he didn't come home and we didn't hear anything else, I started to doubt. Three years later, our daughter was born and I had that postpartum depression. I started fixating on Ricky—I thought if he would just come home, maybe I would feel better. My parents were so worried about me. It was pretty awful."

"Then another postcard arrived," TJ said softly.

"Yes!" Tamara replied. "It was short, like the first, and mailed from somewhere closer, like Lexington, I think. Mostly Ricky just congratulated me on having Jenna and said he knew I'd be a great mom."

"That's sweet," Carlie said.

"It would have been, if I thought it really came from him."

"What made you doubt?" TJ asked.

Tamara glanced out the doorway again, more nervous than ever. "I don't know… Just a feeling. But look, that's not important. What I really came to tell you is I saw that article in the newspaper."

"The one about the investigation?" Carlie asked.

"Yeah. And it said your dad was pretty much the only suspect. Then Dave told me you were checking with some place in Fort Samuel to see if the reverend had been up there around that time."

TJ frowned. "How did Scheuster know I was looking into that?"

Tamara shrugged. "I don't know, but he said that if Reverend Fenton sent that postcard, it meant he knew Ricky was dead and he was trying to cover it up. It meant maybe he was the one who killed him! Well, that's why I had to come back and tell you about the other postcards. Reverend Fenton was a good man, Carlie. He only ever tried to help my brother. There's no way he could have hurt him."

"Thanks," Carlie said. "That means a lot."

"The third postcard I got proved he couldn't have sent them."

"How is that?" TJ asked.

"Because it only arrived three years ago."

Chapter Twelve

"But my father died five years ago!" Carlie exclaimed.

"That's why I had to tell you," Tamara said. "I never told anyone about those other two postcards, not even Dave. I just… I couldn't give my parents any more false hope, you know? My mom was crazy after that first one came—they drove all over, thinking they saw Ricky in this place or that. I got mad at him for tormenting us, so I shoved the postcard in a drawer and tried to forget it."

"But you kept it," Carlie pointed out.

"Mostly by accident. Dave and I moved a couple times, and it literally got boxed up and jumbled around. It took me more than an hour to find it today—that's why I need to hurry. I told Dave I was just coming back home to water the plants. He's at my parents' house with the kids, and he'll start to wonder what's taking so long."

"So you never even told him when the other postcards came?" TJ asked.

She shook her head. "No. By the time the second one came, I was pretty skeptical. I just knew it couldn't be from Ricky. I ripped it up and threw it away. Same thing with the third card. Too bad, huh? Maybe if I had kept that one it would help save your dad's good name, Carlie."

"Were they in the same handwriting as this one?" TJ asked.

"I think so. The third one was sent from someplace I've never heard of. Grenadier Point? Something like that."

"And that was just three years ago?"

"Yes. Our son was in preschool then, and I started working for the county engineer's office. I remember it because...well, Dave and I were kind of going through a rough patch. The last thing I needed was another one of those stupid postcards."

"And you really have no idea who could be sending them?" TJ asked her.

"Honestly, I would tell you if I could. Look, that's all I know. I'm trying to help as much as I can, but I need to go now."

Carlie had a hundred more things to ask her, but TJ seemed content to just let her leave.

"Thanks for coming in," he said with a measure of honest compassion in his voice that Carlie found very refreshing.

"I hope it helps a little," Tamara said, inching toward the door. She gave Carlie a sad half smile. "I remember your dad, Carlie. I know he didn't do this."

"Thanks, Tamara. I'm really, really sorry about... everything."

With another nervous look around the area, she slipped into the hallway and left.

"Careful on that floor out there!" TJ called behind

her, then gave Carlie a guilty cringe. "I guess I'd better go finish cleaning that."

Carlie had to keep herself from laughing out loud. How could this guy be so serious most of the time, then start making faces? He certainly kept her on her toes.

Grabbing a notepad from his desk, she quickly jotted something down.

"Here's my address. It's just a few blocks from here. I'll go home and change. You finish cleaning, then bring the journals. Maybe there'll be some clue in them about who might benefit from convincing Tamara Scheuster that her brother is still alive."

Carlie looked fresh and clean and spaghetti-free when she let him into her apartment. TJ carried the box of journals up the long flight of stairs and found himself in a very spacious living room. The ceilings were high, and one wall was still original brick. Tall windows lined another wall and overlooked Melfield's quaint downtown area.

"Bring the journals in here," she said, leading the way through an arched doorway into a surprisingly large and well-equipped kitchen.

He deposited the box onto one of the chairs at the table. From the delicious smell of garlic and cheese, it appeared she had already started heating up the lasagna. His stomach rumbled in anticipation.

"Good thing I've got something to feed you," she said with a teasing grin. "Sounds like you're about ready to chew off my arm or something."

"I skipped breakfast and probably should have taken lunch a little earlier."

"My mother would scold you. Here, grab a plate and dig in."

She pulled the tray of lasagna out of the oven. He helped himself to a nice portion and was pleasantly surprised when she produced a freshly tossed salad to accompany it. He waited for her to sit at the table, then took his own seat across from her.

There was a moment of silence, and he realized she was privately bowing her head over her food. He hadn't even thought about praying over the meal—he should have. She glanced up and noticed him watching her.

"Sorry, force of habit," she said.

"No, don't be sorry. I shouldn't have just dived in without giving thanks. Now *my* mother would scold me."

"Is she back in Louisville?"

"Yeah. My brother and I have been trying to convince her to move here now that we're both in Melfield. She just won't budge."

"Maybe she's waiting until you're sure you're going to stay here for a while."

"Maybe."

"So, are you?"

"Planning to stay in Melfield? I think so. I like it… so far. Seems like a nice place."

"It is."

"You really don't miss the high life in the big city?"

She had to laugh at that. "My life in the big city consisted almost entirely of me working eighty hours a week and struggling to pay off my student loans. I gave up friends, seeing my mom, having a church family. It was *not* the high life."

"Sometimes, it's like that, starting a career. You have to make sacrifices."

"That's what I kept telling myself," she said, recalling the days before she'd gotten so disillusioned. "It felt like I was working toward a goal, but the goal never got any closer. The harder I worked, the less I had to show for it. I wasn't making a difference... I wasn't helping anyone. Well, after five years, it just started to seem kind of pointless."

"So you left."

"I came home. I thought maybe I could make more of a difference here than I could there. Turns out I made the wrong kind of difference here."

"True, if you hadn't started that work on the church, the body would still be undiscovered. No one would be investigating it. That family would never get closure. Yeah, you made a difference, all right. Seems like a pretty good one."

"Doesn't feel so good to me. I was trying to preserve my father's legacy. It feels more like I ruined it."

"Tamara Scheuster doesn't seem to think so. I know my brother always speaks highly of your father. He touched a lot of lives here in town. I think his legacy will be just fine."

"Not if the bank won't give me that loan. Epiphany Church will just crumble away if someone doesn't step in and fix it."

He'd just taken a big bite of her mother's truly delicious lasagna. If his mouth hadn't been so full, he would have reminded Carlie that Reverend Fenton's legacy wasn't a building, it was the faith that he'd shared. It was the compassion that he'd showed. It was the hope in Carlie's eyes, the way she'd laughed when he dumped spaghetti all over her, the reverence she'd showed when she quietly bowed her head over her meal.

If any man had a legacy to be proud of, it was Carlie Fenton's father.

TJ couldn't say any of that, though. Instead, he mumbled a bit as he managed not to choke on a noodle.

"You're right," she sighed. "Feeling sorry for myself won't help anybody."

He hadn't actually tried to say that, but he supposed it was good advice in the moment.

"What I need to be doing is finding out who actually committed this crime. That's the best way I can help my father. You go ahead and finish. I'll start looking through the journals."

TJ was happy to clean off the rest of his plate, but a part of him was disappointed in the sudden return to business. He had thought he knew everything he needed to know about Carlie Fenton when he first met her and learned she was a lawyer. After several days of literally tripping over her, though, he had begun to realize he hardly knew anything. He'd really started looking forward to their off-topic conversations.

Carlie pulled out a couple of the journals and they discussed where to start. They decided to go through the dates surrounding that supposed Fort Samuel trip eleven years ago. Now that Tamara had been so positive that the postcard couldn't have come from the reverend, Carlie seemed eager to confirm that, by reading her father's entries from that time period.

Since they had the actual postcard in their possession

now, it was easy to pinpoint the date. The postmark was still perfectly legible, even after all this time.

"Do you think it was actually put in the mail on the day that it's postmarked?" she asked, then went on without waiting for his answer. "It could have been dropped off after the mail collection that date. I'd better check Friday and Saturday of that week."

TJ scraped the last bits of cheese off his plate as she flipped through one of the journals.

"Here it is," she announced. "Looks like his Friday journal is all about the yard work he was doing at the time. Gosh, I never realized my dad was so worried about the gutters at the parsonage. He seems kind of obsessed, actually. Are you really supposed to clean gutters three or four times a year?"

"I don't know. We had a landlord and he always took care of that. I live in a condo now, so gutters have never been on my radar."

"Oh, here's one little thing. He mentions a counseling session with 'M.B.'"

"Who is M.B.?" TJ asked.

"I don't know. He usually used initials like that. I think it was for privacy. People didn't always want everyone to know if they were going to the pastor for counseling."

"I can understand that. Well, at least we know if he was at a counseling session with M.B., he couldn't have been off in Fort Samuel, mailing that postcard."

"But he says M.B. didn't show up. Apparently, this has happened before. My dad seems kind of worried about whoever it is."

"Man or woman?"

"Doesn't say—no pronouns. He just says, 'Scheduled counseling with M.B. for this evening, but it was a no-show again. Not sure how to proceed. I left a message to reschedule next week, so we'll see what happens then.' I really don't know who that was."

"Did M.B. reschedule?"

Carlie flipped through more pages. "I don't see any mention of it. Do you think it's important?"

"It shows your dad was clearly here in Melfield on the day that postcard was mailed."

She smiled at that. It was good to see her smile about her father again. "You're right. We know my dad didn't send the postcards. So, who did?"

"Obviously we're not going to find that in his journals. What about going back a year? I'm not suggesting he knew anything about a murder or the body being buried, but maybe something that was going on then might give us more clues to look into."

"True. He could have seen something suspicious and made some note of it."

She dug another book out of the box and flipped through the pages.

"According to the family, the last time they saw Ricky was the middle of April," she said. "I'll start reading a couple weeks before that."

TJ pushed his empty plate back and pulled out his notebook. It really would be remarkable if Carlie found anything useful in the journals, but as long as there was the slightest chance they could learn something from them, it was worth the time they spent here. Besides, TJ was enjoying watching the emotion play over

Carlie's face as she read through her father's day-to-day musings.

At one point she laughed. "Ha! I'd forgotten all about this. I was saving up to buy a necklace I'd seen in the store, but when I went back, it was gone. It turned out my dad got it for me and hid it in my Easter basket. I thought it was stupid to have to go around the house and hunt for an Easter basket when I thought I was already a grown-up, but it was pretty sweet when I found it. I guess my dad had been planning it for a while. He liked to do little things like that."

"It must be nice to know how much he thought about you."

"It is. What about your father, TJ? I don't think you've mentioned him."

"I haven't. He wasn't a part of my life. Matt remembers him a bit, but I don't. He left before I could even walk."

"He left? I'm so sorry. Your mother must be pretty amazing if she raised you both on her own. She must be really proud of how you turned out."

"She is amazing. She wishes I'd turned out a little better, but she's amazing."

"You're head detective for the county sheriff. How much better could she want you to be?"

"You've met my brother, the perfect man of God with the perfect wife and the perfect kids and the perfect life, right?"

Now Carlie laughed like he'd cracked an actual joke. "Oh, I've met your brother and he's a really nice guy, but I promise you, as a preacher's kid who grew up in a parsonage with a whole congregation looking over her shoulder, your brother's life is *not* perfect. They seem to do all right, but I guarantee, it's not perfect."

"To my mother it is. But come on, back to the books. Does your father write about that foundation project? Any funny business going on there?"

"No, he talks about what a pain it is to have that whole section of the churchyard dug up and muddy. He says he's glad they didn't do this ten years earlier, because I would have been playing in the dirt every day." She laughed again at the memories.

Then she leaned in to study a passage. "Oh, he mentions Ricky here. Looks like he's been meeting up with him, helping him with his math homework. Huh, I never knew about that."

"So, he didn't hate the kid. He truly was trying to help him, like Tamara said."

"Yeah. Here's a whole paragraph about how he showed Ricky how to change the oil on the church lawnmower. I never knew any of this!"

"That's the week after Easter. What happened on the days leading up to Ricky's disappearance?"

She scanned through a few entries, then flipped another page. Her fingers stopped tracing the lines, and her smile turned into a confused scowl.

"That's weird."

"What is it?" TJ asked.

She looked up from the book, and her eyes were huge and dark. "The next pages! They're…missing!"

Chapter Thirteen

Carlie shoved the journal over to TJ so he could see for himself. The pages that would have contained her dad's entries for the day before and the two days after Ricky's disappearance were simply not there. It wasn't that her father had made no entries those days, but frayed bits of paper showed pages had actually been torn from the book.

"Someone ripped those days out," TJ noted. "Who would do that?"

"And why? If my father didn't know anything about the murder, what could he have written that needed to be torn out?"

"Maybe he just didn't like what he wrote so he pulled the pages out and started over."

"And it just so happens to be the three most important days of his whole journal-writing career?" Carlie asked, knowing that was too far-fetched even for her to believe. "No, if he tore the pages out, he would have had a reason."

"Are you thinking he might have been trying to protect someone?"

She had been thinking that but hated to say it. "I can't think of any other reason he would have done this. Maybe he knew something that seemed to incriminate someone."

"Your father would have hidden a murder?"

Carlie shook her head and pulled the book back to study it again. "I'm pretty sure he would have reported something like murder. I got a speeding ticket when I was seventeen and he used it as a sermon illustration."

"Even if it was confessed to him in confidence?"

"Even then, he would have gone to the authorities. I don't think he would've noted it in his journal, though. He counseled people all the time about sensitive things—marriage infidelities, addictions, money troubles—but he would have never written in his journal about the private details. If he recorded something, it must have seemed innocuous at the time."

"So, maybe he didn't even know that what he had written incriminated someone."

"And if he didn't know it was incriminating, maybe someone else removed the pages after the fact."

TJ gave her a slow, lopsided smile. "It could very well be our murderer."

She found herself leaning across the table to return his smile. Then she paused. "How would the murderer know what was in my dad's journal, and when would they have had a chance to rip pages out?"

That thought had her stumped. TJ's smile faded. He probably realized—as she did—that if this scenario were true, the murderer was likely someone close to her father. Someone who had access to these journals.

"Who spent time with your father back then? Did he have close friends?"

She thought back through the years. "Well, my parents were friends with several families from church. They'd have Bible study together, go out to dinner together, things like that."

"Did your father keep his journals at home or in his office?"

"At home. Always at home."

"So, who had the most access to your house?"

"It was a parsonage. My parents hosted lots of gatherings and prayer groups. People were in and out all the time. Everyone knew where his desk was at home—he kept his journals in it."

TJ nodded. "So you're saying any of the church members could have potentially torn the pages out."

"Other people, too. Dad was involved in a couple civic groups and community organizations—so was Mom. Their groups met at our house. Like I said, people were in and out all the time."

"Not to mention, you and your mother both had constant access to the journals."

"So my *mother* is a suspect now?"

"And you, of course."

She glared at him, but he simply laughed at her.

"Look, I'm just pointing out that any number of people could have accessed that journal and altered it," he said.

His laughter turned to a deep sigh that indicated he felt as frustrated as she did. For a few minutes, she'd thought they'd actually cleared her father. These journals were simply supposed to confirm his innocence.

Now the very absence of these pages seemed to add suspicion.

"I just wish I could remember any details from back then," she complained. "I should have paid more attention."

"You were a teenager. And as you've said over and over, no one really thought Ricky was dead. As far as you knew, he was a juvenile delinquent who ran away. It probably felt like good riddance."

"It sounds awful to say that now, but yeah, it kind of did. He was causing so much trouble, but I should have been more understanding."

TJ reached across the table and took her hand. It startled her, but the most surprising thing about his unexpected touch was that she didn't instinctively pull her hand away. She welcomed his friendly gesture.

"It wasn't your responsibility to fix things back then," TJ said.

"But now my father looks guilty again!"

"No, he doesn't. Think about it. Tamara Scheuster says that third postcard came just three years ago. Your father couldn't have had anything to do with that."

"But she didn't keep the card, did she? We've got no proof, just an entry in my dad's day planner that says he might have gone to Fort Samuel on the very weekend that first card was mailed."

"We've got that card now, don't we? Let's compare it. Does it match the writing in your dad's journals?"

He had a point. She released his hand and took the postcard as he pulled it from his pocket. Even from a distance, she knew the handwriting was not even close to her father's. No one could mistake it—the postcard was composed by someone else.

"It's not my dad's writing."

"No, it's not," he agreed. "So whose could it be?"

"The obvious guess would be whoever Ricky had the most trouble with. But everyone seems to think that was my dad."

"Tamara didn't think so. She said your dad only tried to help him."

"What about Scheuster and Mitch?" Carlie offered. "Do you think one of them did it? Could they have sent the postcards?"

"I can probably find something with Scheuster's handwriting on it so we could compare," TJ said.

Carlie suddenly felt brighter. It honestly made sense that they should consider the two boys. And she knew where they could find a sample of Mitch's writing, too.

"I've got everyone's handwriting," she said. "They signed my sophomore yearbook. All three of them did—Scheuster, Mitch and Ricky. They wrote goofy stuff. One of them even wrote a poem. We can compare those entries to that postcard."

TJ was smiling again. "Now, that's good detective work. All right, bring out the yearbook."

"I can't."

"Why not?"

"It isn't here. It's in my mom's storage unit."

"Well, Miss Fenton, it looks like we're taking another trip down memory lane. Would you like to drive, or should I?"

TJ ended up taking his car, since it had been parked right outside Carlie's apartment and, after all, this was official business. He pulled away from the curb and made a turn at the next traffic light. Carlie clutched the card, silently reading it over and studying the postmark.

TJ had done the same thing. Nothing about the postcard stuck out as remarkable, other than the somewhat sloppy penmanship and the obvious grammar errors. It was easy to believe a troubled eighteen-year-old boy had scribbled it quickly. It was much harder to believe an educated professional, like Reverend Fenton, could have written it.

Still, TJ knew there would be questions. So far, the postcard had not entered into the investigation, since he had not actually had it as evidence. Now it would be. It would be studied and scrutinized. If they did find a handwriting match for it in Carlie's yearbook today, TJ would turn it all over to a lab so the writing could be confirmed by specialists. TJ knew all too well the importance of getting expert analysis rather than relying on one cop's opinion.

The storage unit was on the outskirts of town, and they were nearly there when a call came over TJ's radio. Another burglary had been reported and the officers on scene requested his assistance. It seemed to be connected to a couple similar cases he'd been investigating, so it was important for him to be involved.

"I'm sorry. I need to make a detour," he said to Carlie. "Do you mind riding out there with me? It shouldn't take too long."

"That's fine. I won't be in the way?"

"No, I just need to talk to the property owners, make sure we have all the information we need. Sounds like they were hit by the same guys who've been breaking into barns and garages all over the county lately."

"I saw something about that in the newspaper," Carlie said. "Any idea who's doing this?"

He shrugged. "The thieves seem to know what they're after, so that suggests familiarity. I'm still trying to figure out what the burglaries have in common."

"You don't think it's some kind of organized operation, do you?"

"No. Personally, I think they're local kids."

"Kids? You mean teenagers?"

"And other young people. Look around, Carlie. Melfield might be a nice little town, but there's not a lot going on here. Not a lot of career options. You were able to get out, to go get an education and build a career for yourself. But you had to do that outside of Melfield. Kids who don't have those opportunities sometimes turn to other alternatives."

"So they choose crime?"

"Occasionally. Just look at your friend Ricky. He had stuff going on in his life and didn't know how to deal with it. What did he do? He started making trouble. It got him attention."

"Obviously, the wrong kind of attention."

"It happens all the time, sadly. It's just too bad there aren't more resources to help these young people. They mess up a couple times, and it just snowballs. There's no way for them to make a fresh start."

"When things were getting broken around the church and we all knew Ricky had done it, my dad worried that the situation would get worse for him. I guess it did."

"I've talked to the sheriff about setting up some kind of program for kids, something that would help them break away from bad influences and get interested in their futures."

"That would be great."

"Doing it right would be a little bit more than the sheriff's office can handle, I'm afraid. Like I said, there just aren't enough resources or facilities around here."

"Too bad. My dad would have supported something like that."

"I know my brother would, too. Maybe it'll happen someday, but probably not soon enough for the ones involved in these burglaries. Well, here's the address. Do you mind waiting in the car? I shouldn't be long."

"I'll be fine," she assured him as he pulled the car to a stop next to a cruiser parked at a farmhouse. "Do what you can. Maybe you'll actually catch these kids before they get themselves in worse trouble...or wind up like Ricky."

Carlie enjoyed the fresh country air flowing through the open windows. TJ had offered to keep the car running for her, but that seemed wasteful. He'd parked in the shade, and the breeze today was wonderful. With the birds singing overhead and the soothing rustle of swaying willow branches, she was perfectly comfortable.

TJ had brought them to a very picturesque farm. She'd recognized the name on the mailbox as that of a prominent farming family in the area, but she couldn't recall ever meeting them. It appeared the burglary must've occurred in one of the many big red outbuildings on the site. A uniformed officer was standing in the wide doorway of the building out behind the house, talking to a middle-aged couple. TJ had joined them and seemed to be taking notes.

At one point, he pulled out his phone and took a call. He stepped away from the others, and Carlie could just catch glimpses of him as he paced in and out of view, obviously deep in conversation. For a while, his hand gestures became quite animated, as if he were expressing strong opinions about something, but she was too far away to hear whatever any of them were saying. Eventually, he ended the call and rejoined the others, asking questions and taking more notes.

She leaned back in the seat and wondered how much longer he'd be. Her assistant back at her office knew she'd be out most of the afternoon, so Carlie wasn't worried about missing any appointments. She did generally try to keep up with email, though, so she pulled out her phone to see if anything pressing needed attention. Flipping through her messages, her fingers fumbled and she dropped her phone.

Naturally, it didn't just fall onto her lap or even onto her feet. It slipped down between the seat and the center console that housed what appeared to be an entire computer system. Careful not to push any buttons or bump any important gadgets, Carlie squirmed to fit her hand into the gap between seat and console. She felt her phone wedged against something.

It was a book. She could just barely get her fingers over it to slide it up through the gap with her phone. A tight squeeze, but she finally got it. Her phone dropped onto her seat and she was left holding the book.

No, it wasn't just a book, it was a Bible. Why did it surprise her to learn TJ carried his Bible in his cruiser?

Everything about him said he was a man who cared about right and wrong, who lived by a deeply moral code. He'd grown up in the church, he'd told her. They shared that in common. Naturally, his faith was an important part of his life.

It felt like an invasion of privacy, though, to be holding his Bible. The gold-embossed letters on it—TJ Douglas—reminded her that her own Bible was getting dusty on a shelf back at her apartment. She would simply tuck his away, back where he'd had it.

As she shifted it in her hand, something between the pages slipped out. A photograph. She picked it up and couldn't help but look at it. The smiling face of a young woman with dark hair and bright eyes greeted her. Instinctively, she turned it over. "TJ—all my love forever—Rissa" was written in loopy, felt-tip pen. There was even a little heart drawn carefully in the corner. It seemed intensely personal.

Carlie's own heart slammed into her chest. It was very wrong to be going through TJ's private things this way. She should put the photo back into the Bible and shove it down between the seat and the console, where she'd found it.

She couldn't take her eyes off the words on the back of the photo, though. "All my love forever." Obviously, this was someone very special to TJ. He'd not mentioned her, and Carlie instinctively felt she had no right to wonder about her.

But she did wonder, of course. Who was Rissa? Did TJ still have all her love forever? That would be quite a commitment.

Not that he'd ever given Carlie any reason to think he

couldn't be promised somewhere. They hadn't dated, or anything. Her only interactions with TJ had been strictly professional, working with him on this case and trying to prove her father's innocence. When they'd shared a meal or laughed together, it had only ever been over this shared enterprise.

So why couldn't she get that woman's face out of her mind? She didn't want to think about her, wonder about who she was or what she meant to TJ. That was none of Carlie's business, after all. She really shouldn't feel anything about some stranger who loved TJ forever or any of the women he might interact with on a personal level.

She just couldn't stop, though. All sorts of scenarios flashed through her mind. Maybe Rissa was just an old friend—who had pledged undying love and drawn hearts on her photo. Maybe Rissa was a cousin or just some close family friend—who had pledged undying love and drawn hearts on her photo. Maybe Rissa was some minor celebrity and this was how she gave out autographs—by pledging undying love and drawing hearts on her photo. No matter what scenario Carlie thought of—and she came up with several—they were all defeated by the words on the back of that picture and the sweet smile on the woman's face.

Whoever Rissa was, she had loved TJ enough to declare it in writing. He had responded by lovingly keeping her image in his most sacred possession. There weren't many other things this could mean besides the obvious: TJ was deeply, romantically involved with a beautiful woman named Rissa.

And Carlie was jealous.

How ridiculous was that? She barely even knew TJ.

Sure, he was growing on her—slowly—but she certainly didn't care enough about him to be jealous of some woman in a photo. Did she?

The very idea left her feeling flustered and off balance. She'd been so focused on work, so busy trying to look out for herself, that she hadn't even thought about dating anyone for quite a long time. How could she suddenly, after less than a week of working with TJ, be having such unexpected and confusing feelings about him?

She couldn't, of course. She wouldn't let herself. She would forget she ever saw that photo. She'd put it back and return the Bible to the—

"Hey, where did you find that?"

TJ yanked his door open and glared at her, the Bible on her lap and the photo in her hand.

"I… I dropped my phone and it got wedged in with your Bible," she stammered quickly. "Then this photo fell out. I was just putting it back."

TJ didn't wait for her to do that. He got inside and reached his hand out. She gave him the Bible and laid the photo on top of it. His expression was cold and unreadable as he tucked the picture into the pages and then slid the Bible under his seat.

"Who is she?" Carlie asked, though she'd been trying to convince herself not to.

"A friend of mine."

"Does she live in Louisville?"

"Not anymore. Strap in. I've got to go back to the office. I'll drop you off at your place."

"But what about going to the storage unit to get the yearbook?"

"I can't. They need me back at the sheriff's office right now."

"Okay. I guess I'll get the yearbook on my own and compare the handwriting…"

"No, I'd better take the journals and the postcard with me. The day planners, too. They're considered evidence now."

"Now? They weren't before?"

"Not really. There wasn't any actual connection to the body."

"But there is now?"

"Yes. The coroner just turned in his report."

She waited. A couple seconds ticked by before he continued.

"We've got a positive ID. It's Ricky LeMaster, all right. And he was murdered."

Chapter Fourteen

TJ felt like a heel. He'd been too cold toward Carlie. She was hurt, he could tell. If he were a decent guy, he would have told her the truth.

But he couldn't do that, could he? Sheriff Villa had been very clear about that. Now that they had a positive ID, the case could truly proceed. Villa insisted on being more involved now, and he didn't like the idea of sharing ongoing investigation details with Carlie. Nothing TJ said could convince the man that Reverend Fenton was not their primary suspect.

TJ had tried to explain that there was no real evidence to indicate Carlie's father had anything to do with the murder, but the sheriff was adamant. TJ was to stop working with Carlie and cease including her in the investigation. Whatever documentation she had that might have a connection to the case, TJ was to take possession of it immediately. If she didn't like that, he would just have to get a judge to issue a search warrant.

He didn't figure showing up at her apartment with a warrant would do much for soothing Carlie's hurt feelings. Fortunately, she'd given him the journals and the day planners without question. Well, she'd asked a few questions, but she hadn't complained when he'd refused to answer. Not too much anyway.

He should have known letting himself get close to her was a mistake. This was a criminal case—it always had been. Even if there was not a shred of evidence to incriminate her father, the fact still remained that somehow a body had been buried at his church, under his watch. That automatically made him a suspect.

Now TJ was driving back to the sheriff's office with a stack of papers in the reverend's own handwriting that could very well include details about his disagreements with Ricky and the anger he felt over the boy's treatment of his daughter. Worse, the very pages surrounding the days of Ricky's disappearance had been intentionally ripped out. TJ had no doubt what the sheriff would make of that.

TJ had the postcard, of course, but the author of that still had to be determined. As for the other two— especially the one that could be proven *not* to have come from Reverend Fenton—they had been conveniently destroyed. Unless he could positively identify the sender of the first one, TJ knew it wouldn't take much imagination to suggest the reverend had penned that postcard with intentionally flawed grammar and disguised his handwriting. It was an outlandish theory, but it would be very difficult to disprove. Especially with that trip to Fort Samuel listed in his day planner.

It would be entirely too easy to latch on to these elements and consider them incriminating. At this point, the sheriff was eager for a solution and might grasp at any convenient clues. TJ, however, was not eager to get back to the office and discuss it with him. When they spoke over the phone a half hour ago while he was on the burglary call, the sheriff had made it very clear he wanted this case wrapped up quickly.

TJ knew that meant he would not be encouraged to follow other leads. It would break Carlie's heart that the sheriff was ready to use her dad as a scapegoat. But what could TJ do about it?

What he should do was call her and explain. He should apologize to her, too, but he couldn't do either. Villa was waiting and TJ had to do his duty.

He hauled the box of journals up to his office, then took a deep breath to calm his anger and grabbed the phone to call the first-floor administrative assistant.

"You can let the sheriff know I'm back in my office anytime he wants to see me."

"Sure thing, Detective," she replied cheerfully.

TJ leaned back in his chair and rubbed his forehead. He shouldn't have gotten upset at Carlie for pulling out that photo, either. It had just caught him off guard, that was all. The more he'd worked this case—the more he'd worked with Carlie—the more he'd really tried not to think of Rissa. He'd tried to put that whole tragic episode behind him.

That seemed to be beyond his ability, though. The nature of this case only made him remember more of the pain and frustration he'd tried to forget. He hated that feeling of helplessness, of not quite being good enough. He wanted to help Carlie. He wanted to see her get the justice she needed, not just for her friend Ricky but to preserve her father's legacy. More than anything, he wanted to feel that his efforts were causing some good in the world.

Right now, it seemed he was just as powerless as he had been before. Justice might be out of reach for Carlie, just as it had been for Rissa. Reverend Fenton might end up taking the blame for a murder TJ was sure he had not committed. Carlie would be stuck carrying that weight.

He knew only too well how heavy that weight was.

Sheriff Villa interrupted his thoughts. "So, it looks like the thugs that hit the Kessler farm last night are the same ones we've been after?"

TJ glanced up to find the sheriff in his doorway again. "You didn't have to come up here. I would've come down to your office."

Villa dismissed that with a shrug. "That's fine. Think we'll get these guys?"

"I think so," TJ replied, pulling out his notebook. "I've got some ideas on the case. It seems there are a couple things consistent from one break-in to the next. That gives me a place to start, at least. Want me to brief you?"

"No, I'll catch up later. Right now we've got to talk about the Fenton case."

"You mean the LeMaster case. The boy who was murdered was Ricky LeMaster. There's no solid Fenton connection at all."

"Look, TJ, I know you're friendly with the girl, but people want details on this case."

"Once we have them, we'll let the public know."

"Yes, usually we don't go around talking about ongoing investigations. But when the case is so old—so cold—and the prime suspect has been dead for five years, it's not like there's a real reason to sit on what we're finding."

"We haven't found much yet. We only just got the positive ID this afternoon."

"Yep, and I've already sent the press release to the newspaper. It'll probably be on the front page again."

"Is that wise?"

"You're questioning how I run my office?"

"No, sir. I just wonder if maybe we should have waited on that until the family could be fully notified, that's all."

"They're notified. I've been keeping Scheuster up to date on all the developments. And he's been keeping me informed, too. He was pretty tight with the LeMaster kid back then, you know. He had a few things to say about the boy's run-ins with the minister."

It seemed odd that Scheuster would be offering information to the sheriff and not directly to TJ. What did Scheuster know that hadn't already been brought up when Ricky first disappeared? TJ didn't like the sound of this.

"What did he have to say?" TJ asked. "I should maybe call him and get a statement."

"I've got his statement. There are other things I need you to be doing."

"Oh? What is that?"

"I'm heading you back to your old stomping grounds. I've talked to a buddy of mine at the Louisville metro PD, and they've been seeing a wave of items being brought in from rural areas and fenced through local pawnshops. Maybe our local thieves are unloading things there. So I need you to head to Louisville for a couple days and take a look at what they've picked up so far, see if there's anything that can tie into our string of burglaries here."

"I suppose I can make some time for that next week, but—"

"No, I need you to go now. I told him you'd be there first thing in the morning. Take the whole weekend, catch up with old friends and maybe hit some of the hot spots where stolen goods have been turning up. You know, go through what they've got in evidence, all that."

"But sir, I really need to be here, working on *this* case!"

"I could take you off this case permanently, if you want," the sheriff threatened. "I need you on these burglaries. Ricky LeMaster isn't going to get any more dead if you take off for a couple days."

"Okay, I'll go if that's what you need me to do."

"It is. I'll shoot the details to you in an email."

"All right. Is that all you needed?"

"It is." Villa gave him a dismissive smile, then turned to go. He leaned back in at the last moment. "Oh, and don't forget what we talked about. Keep a clear head with Carlie Fenton. She stays out of this investigation, got it?"

"Yes, you made that perfectly clear, sir."

The sheriff left, and TJ grumbled under his breath. He didn't appreciate being pulled off a homicide case and sent to track down stolen farm tools. What was Villa up to anyway? Did he have some vested interest in shutting down the LeMaster investigation and closing the case?

TJ couldn't think of any. Villa was apparently from the Melfield area, but he'd been working for a sheriff's office somewhere in Indiana for twenty years before he returned here. As far as TJ knew, he hadn't been back when Ricky disappeared. It didn't seem likely Sheriff Villa had reason to hide anything regarding Ricky LeMaster.

Unless maybe he did? TJ would have to look into that as carefully as possible. Unfortunately, it would have to wait. Villa apparently wanted him in Louisville over the weekend. Well, it would be nice to see some of his friends there, and of course, his mom would insist he stay at her place while he was in town. He'd better call and give her a heads-up.

He ought to call Carlie, too, and let her know where Villa was sending him. But that might seem like they really were working as a team, as if he had some right to expect her to care about where he was and what he was doing. The sheriff had made it very clear that he was not to consider Carlie anything more than a possible person of interest for the case. If he didn't want to cross any lines or even give the appearance of it, he'd better heed Villa's instructions.

He'd send Carlie a text on Saturday to let her know he wouldn't be meeting her after church on Sunday. She'd understand. He hoped.

Carlie just couldn't understand. TJ had taken her home and picked up the journals and day planners, with hardly more than ten words. They'd had such a good afternoon up until that point. Now he'd been cold and even seemed angry with her.

Had it really upset him so much that she'd found that photo in his Bible? It had been a breach of privacy, she got that. But she'd tried to explain it was an accident—she really hadn't tried to pry into his things or his personal life. What could have possibly flipped the switch from friendly banter to cool distance between them so quickly?

It must've been something she'd done. Well, nothing she could do about it now. She'd try calling TJ later. Maybe he'd talk about it then. In the meanwhile, she had a couple free hours before dinnertime. Why not go to her mom's storage unit alone and get that yearbook as she had planned? It was true, TJ had taken the postcard, but she had a fairly good memory of the writing on it. She could at least look at the books and let TJ know if she thought there was a possible match. Surely, he'd want to know that, even if he was angry with her.

The late afternoon sun was still hot, and Carlie hoped she wouldn't have to spend too much time in the stifling storage unit when she got there. Everything seemed to be just as they'd left it on Tuesday, so Carlie had a pretty good idea where to start hunting for the boxes that might contain books from her old bedroom.

Squeezing past the open cartons they'd been looking through two days ago, she bumped into a lamp. The same one her mother had knocked over when they'd found her here. Like mother, like daughter, she figured. Carlie righted it and continued on to the collection of boxes she wanted to investigate.

"Carlie's Room" was written on them in black marker. Prying them open one at a time, she was struck by nostalgia, regret and a hundred other emotions. It was like encountering an old friend and not even realizing how much you had missed them until you saw their face once again.

She found the usual things one might expect from a teenage girl's bedroom: lots of trinkets and keepsakes, the trophy from her one year of dance competition, a rainbow of 4-H ribbons for the projects she'd entered at the county fair each year, and the ragged teddy bear she had snuggled since toddler years. She pulled him out of the box and set him aside.

Ah, here were the books from her shelves. Digging through stories about pirates, tales about dragons and an entire series about orphan ballerinas solving mysteries, she finally found the high school yearbooks. She wiped sweat off her cheek and hauled them out.

It was just too hot to look at them here, so she bundled them all under her arm and scooped up the teddy bear. She'd take it all home and go through the books there, with air-conditioning and a nice, comfy chair. On her way through the cluttered belongings, she bumped the lamp once again.

This time the fixture tipped all the way over and fell to the floor. It was mostly metal and there was no bulb in it, so nothing broke, but she was forced to put all her things down so she could move the lamp out of her way. As she picked it up, an envelope fell out that had been tucked inside the shade.

No, she realized. Not an envelope. Folded paper. Curious, she unfolded the sheets, only to nearly drop them in surprise.

These were the pages missing from her father's journal! The only possible person who could have torn them out and hidden them here was…her mother. What on earth had Mom found in them that she'd needed to rip them out and hide them?

TJ finished putting the rest of the things he'd need for his trip into his travel bag. He zipped it up and tossed it on the floor near the doorway. He'd told his mom to expect him around eight tonight, so he needed to get going.

It just didn't feel right, leaving Melfield in the middle of a homicide case. For a moment, it had felt like he and Carlie were just about at a breakthrough. Maybe if they'd gotten her yearbook, they could have matched up the handwriting. Maybe that would be the one clue they needed to figure the whole thing out.

Instead, TJ was preparing to head off and scope out pawnshops two hours away.

He glanced at the newspaper sitting on his table. His copy of the *Melfield Mid-Day* had been delivered right on time, just after three o'clock. Sure enough, the front-page headline declared that the body had been identified as Ricky LeMaster. Obviously, Sheriff Villa had sent that press release the moment he got the coroner's report. Very likely, the newspaper had known it was coming and saved space for it, rushing it to press in time for the early afternoon printing. The same reporter who had sensationalized Carlie's father's involvement had done even more of the same in this article.

This time, the man's anonymous source declared that Ricky was in a fight with someone the day before he disappeared. Apparently, he'd come to school with a black eye. No one could recall who he'd been fighting with, but someone who claimed to be a former classmate of his remembered Ricky talking about meeting the minister for tutoring after school. There was a highly embellished rehashing of the parking lot dispute between Ricky and the reverend, and it was obvious what the public was supposed to infer from all that.

TJ shoved the paper into one of the pockets of his bag. He hated the way the reporter was twisting the facts, but he needed to read the article carefully to stay on top of whatever misinformation was being distributed to the public. He'd likely have some fires to put out when he came back.

His investigation division was a small one, and he had only three detectives under him, but he'd left word for them to be on the lookout for anything that might be helpful. Unfortunately, they were all currently wrapping up other cases. No doubt Sheriff Villa would keep them busy with those over the weekend.

Why was the man so worried about anyone turning up new information? Would it be so very bad if they had a few other clues to follow, clues that did not directly point to Carlie's dad? Sure, TJ understood that it would be great to wrap up the case neat and tidy within such a short time, but if they weren't 100 percent certain of the reverend's guilt—and TJ wasn't—how could they sit back and ignore the possibility that there was a killer on the loose somewhere?

His phone buzzed. He glanced at it. Carlie was calling him.

She'd probably seen the article. He should take her call. But what could he tell her? The only news he had right now was not good. He just couldn't bring himself to let her know how hard it was going to be to make sure her father was treated fairly. He couldn't crush her like that.

So he declined her call. Better to have her angry at him for being a jerk than for her to be angry at the whole justice system for failing so miserably. TJ wondered why he wasn't used to it by now.

Turning off his phone, he dropped it into his pocket and locked the door behind him as he left.

The call went to voice mail. Why didn't TJ pick up? She could only assume he was tied up with something, but an annoying little worry made her wonder if he was avoiding her.

She really wanted to tell him what she'd found. After she'd discovered the ripped papers in the storage unit, she'd been a bit apprehensive about reading them. Well, she finally had. Twice now.

They contained nothing that would incriminate her father. She had learned a great deal from them, though. The pages were still laid out on her coffee table. She picked up the first page and scanned it again. The journal entry was for Thursday, May 2. The first part of the entry mentioned the Bible verses he'd used for his devotional at the nursing home that day and mentioned what the family had for dinner, but there was nothing of interest. The entry continued, though, with an addendum apparently added the next day.

Those boys were at it again. Gone to bed, woken up by noises in the church parking lot. Hard to see from the windows, but headlights for sure. Two cars driving around, tearing up the gravel. All that construction equipment is still out there—can't have them tearing up that.

I went out to see what was going on. Found R.L. with M.B. and D.S., the three musketeers. They'd obviously been partying—D was so bad off he seemed mostly passed out in the back seat

of the car. I reminded them it was too late for this
behavior and they shouldn't be driving in their
state. M and R assured me only D had been drinking. They were just hanging out, waiting for him
to sober up before taking him home. I threatened
to call parents and they didn't like that, promised
to be quiet and get D home safely.

I was pretty sure R, at least, was telling the truth
about not drinking, so I let him go if he promised
to drive the other two. They agreed to take R's car
and come back for D's truck in the morning. I left
them to sort it out but told them if they weren't
gone in ten minutes, I'd call their parents.

I went back in and watched out the front window. They revved the engine, hot-rodded a bit, and
I heard some squabbling, but it wasn't long and
they tore out of there. Had one of my headaches
by then, so slept in my chair in the den for a while.

The entry for the next day made no mention of
this, except to say that D's truck had been picked up
and the parking lot gravel showed some signs of kids
hot-rodding but no real damage. No matter how many
times she read it, Carlie just couldn't see how any of
that incriminated her father. It matched up with the
story she remembered from the time—the boys said
they'd been out partying with Ricky, went home, and
he'd disappeared the next day.

Why had her mother torn the pages out? Was there
something here that Carlie was missing? She just didn't
see it. She really wanted to tell TJ about it, though, and
it was more than a little frustrating that he hadn't re-

turned her call when she'd left a message at his office and now when she'd tried his cell phone.

It was tempting to plop in a chair and eat ice cream for dinner, but that wouldn't help anything, either. Putting her shoes back on, she trotted up the block to the little sandwich shop and brought something home for a light dinner. The newspaper had been delivered and was lying by her front door, rolled up and bound with a rubber band. She grabbed it and trotted back upstairs.

Sitting at the table with her sandwich, she unrolled the paper and was once again infuriated by the lead article. How on earth did this reporter get all his information so quickly? He must truly have an inside line at the sheriff's office. She muttered under her breath as she read about her father's supposed "altercation" with Ricky. There was a thinly veiled hint that perhaps he had given the boy a black eye, too.

Angry, she threw the paper across the room. It landed, open to the next page. Even from where she sat, she could read the headline of another article: "Sheriff Investigates String of Local Break-ins." Maybe the awful reporter would try to pin those on her father, too.

She grumbled at herself for being so quick to expect the worst. Since when was she the sort of person who threw things in an angry outburst? Leaving her sandwich, she went to retrieve the paper and find out just what information the article contained. TJ's name stood out to her from the break-in article. She read what they had to say about him.

Lt. Det. TJ Douglas, head of investigations with the local sheriff's office, has stated that he has

several leads. He will be traveling to Louisville
over the weekend to work with detectives there
who are assisting in the investigation.

Well, that explained why she hadn't heard back from
him. He was traveling. Okay, that made her feel a little
bit better. It would've been nice if he'd told her, though.
He obviously knew ahead of time, since the newspaper
was able to publish it already.

She sighed and was just about to take another bite of
her sandwich when her phone sounded. She rushed into
the other room to fish it out of her purse and answer.

"This is Kim Daley, from Melfield Mortgage."

"Oh, hello, Kim. I was hoping to hear from you this
week."

"I thought I'd just better get in touch to let you know
that we've been aware of the situation at the church
building."

"Yeah, that's obviously not at all what any of us expected to find there, huh?"

"No. It wasn't, and, well, I'm sorry, but we've re-
viewed the situation, and I'm afraid, at this time, we
are just not going to be able to move forward with any
loan for that property."

"But I'm sure things will get sorted out soon! Maybe
you can just put the application on hold, give me some
time and then we can start the process all over when
it's not so...crazy."

"No, I'm sorry. It's not just the situation. The bank
feels that given the extensive work needed on the facility and your limited credit history, it's just too much
of a risk to expect your business to support such debt."

"I see."

"I hope you understand. It's nothing personal. Maybe once all this is sorted out, we can work together on something less ambitious."

"Right."

Kim made some light chatter about how great it was to meet Carlie and how she hoped everything went well with all her future endeavors, but it was clear the matter was truly settled. Carlie got off the phone, feeling defeated. Her father was being raked over the coals of public opinion, her dream for his legacy had fallen flat and TJ was off somewhere, chasing teenagers on a crime spree.

Well, this was turning out to be a wonderful day. She had been going to call her mother to ask about these pages, but no. She would absolutely not do that tonight. She wouldn't bother going through that yearbook, either. What difference would it make if she did identify the handwriting on that postcard? TJ wasn't answering her calls to hear about it. Learning anything more about the case while she was so utterly helpless to save her father's good name would just make her even more depressed.

No, the only thing to do tonight would be change into her pajamas early and finish off that tub of chocolate fudge chunk ice cream she had in the freezer. Maybe she should've just done that to start with, instead of reading the newspaper. Then, at least, she wouldn't know where TJ had gone.

And she wouldn't spend the weekend wondering if he was hanging out with Rissa.

Chapter Fifteen

Carlie had spent Friday and Saturday alternately feeling sorry for herself and being angry at just about everyone. She'd called her mom on Friday, only to find she was interrupting another golf outing, so could she call back? She'd called back, only to get her mom's voice mail. She'd called again on Saturday and explained her concerns about the articles in the newspaper and was shocked when, again, the woman who had been her father's life partner for twenty-five years had shrugged off the slander as unimportant.

She'd told Carlie she was overreacting. Carlie had been so upset by her mother's dismissal that she'd forgotten to even mention being turned down for the loan or to ask questions about the pages ripped out of the journal. This was exactly why their relationship had been so shallow and cool for so long.

Her mom didn't seem to care about anything anymore. She just wanted to keep busy and not have to talk about things or think about things. Maybe Carlie had been okay with that when she was struggling through law school or when she was working grueling hours to get ahead in her career, but she wanted more for her life now.

She wanted an honest connection with her mother. They'd had that once—she remembered it clearly. There'd been a time when Carlie could've told her mother everything, gone to her with every problem. And Mom would have dropped what she was doing to listen. Mom would have cared.

Now, her mother was too busy to even sit with Carlie in church.

Carlie entered the sanctuary at Faith Community Church on Sunday morning and felt instantly out of place. She knew many of the faces, of course, but it didn't feel like her church home. It didn't feel like Epiphany. It didn't feel *right*.

She noticed her mother up at the front of the church, mingling with the other choir members as they took their places in the seating behind the altar. She was smiling, looking very attractive in a coral-colored dress, with her hair freshly styled. Even after all the years and all the tragedy, she was still a beautiful woman who brightened every room she went into. Carlie couldn't remember the last time her mother had dropped by to brighten any room in her home, though.

Glancing around, Carlie looked for a seat. She saw her mom's special friend, Bob, sitting with some of their golfing buddies. Carlie was *not* going to sit over there.

She noticed the pastor's wife, Wendy Douglas, greeting everyone with a smile and managing to keep the adorable Douglas children in perfect order as they made their way up to their usual pew in the front. Maybe TJ was right—they did seem about as perfect as anyone could be. It was annoying. Carlie was not going to go sit by them.

Then she noticed TJ. He was alone, at the far end of a pew. It looked like he could be ready to dart out at a moment's notice or leap up and take charge of any situation that might arise. She paused in the aisle. He'd got his hair cut over the past two days—it looked really good. *He* looked really good.

He must've felt her looking at him, because his head turned her way. Their eyes met, and a slow smile spread on his face. Carlie's breath caught. Was he happy to see her? She tried not to look quite so happy to see him.

She failed miserably when he tipped his head toward the empty seat beside him. To get over to that side of the church, she'd have to go past two of the little old ladies who always wanted to tell her how much they missed her father. And to get up to TJ's pew she'd have to risk being sucked into conversation with Margie Sanders, who was just two rows behind him. But the surprise of seeing him there was too hard to overcome. She hadn't thought he'd be back, had thought that perhaps he'd forgotten their plan to attend church and meet up with Mrs. Brown afterward. But he hadn't. He was here.

She *would* go sit with him.

"Hi," he said after she'd made it through the gauntlet. "I'm glad you're here."

"I'm surprised *you're* here," she replied. "How was Louisville?"

"It was...informative," he said. "I'm glad to be back."

The organ started playing, and there wasn't time for more small talk. It nearly killed her not to ask him what had been so informative. Did he find any of the stolen items? Did he catch the burglars? Did he find out Rissa had downgraded her emotions to "casual friends forever"?

She couldn't think about that, though. This was church, after all. She'd come here to worship, and she would do her best to put her mind where it ought to be.

The choir's first song was as wonderful as her mom had said it would be. The scripture reading was from Colossians. At first Carlie was listening out of duty and respect, but she realized the verses spoke to some of the very things she'd been wrestling with—the struggle between human nature and a life more fully guided by faith. Had TJ been telling Pastor Matt about her? Or maybe the minister's scripture selection had not been directed by human intervention at all.

Matt began his sermon by motioning toward TJ. Carlie poked him with her elbow and chuckled. He seemed to hate being singled out.

Pastor Matt said that, as a detective, TJ put on certain things in the morning before he went to the department. He put on his gun, his protective vest and any other item he might require for what he'd be doing. If he tried to work wearing the wrong sort of equipment, he might not be able to do his job.

Matt compared this to the scripture he'd just read about the need to put off things like evil and covetousness. He went on to read the verses that followed, instructing people to put on kindness, humility and patience. He stressed one verse especially: "And above all these things put on charity, which is the bond of perfectness."

Carlie felt those words in her soul. She realized that for too long now, she'd been putting on an appearance, but she'd not really been focused on what she should be. She'd come back to Melfield searching for the bond she'd felt with her past, but she hadn't put on the things she needed. She'd not told her mother how she really felt, she'd not devoted any of her time to growing closer to God, and the first thing she'd done when she met TJ was to be distrustful and have a bad attitude.

Charity meant godly love. Could she put on a more loving mindset? It would certainly help her build a deeper relationship with her mother. She might even learn to give Bob a chance. And what about TJ? Could she put on a more trusting and supportive attitude toward him?

She suddenly noticed the weight of the ornate-silver cross pendant she wore today. Reaching for it, she traced the familiar shape, reminding herself what it stood for. Yes, because of all that it meant, she *could* put on the sort of charitable love that would bind things in perfectness. She made a silent vow.

Glancing up, she noticed TJ watching her. She didn't look away, though. Things were going to be better between them—she would do her part to make that happen.

Pastor Matt's voice echoed around them. "Above all these things, put on charity—these are the words of our Lord. So I ask you all, what will you put on today?"

He let the question hang in the air, then closed out his sermon and invited everyone to stand for the closing hymn. It was an old favorite. The congregation sang with enthusiastic harmonies, and Carlie couldn't help but feel herself transported back to childhood. She could almost hear her father's rich baritone belting out the sacred verses.

Actually, it wasn't her father singing the hymn in her mind—she could hear TJ beside her. He'd been silent through the rest of the service, but this time, he was singing along. He seemed to know every word, too. His voice blended with all those around them, and Carlie realized that all her anger, all the years she'd avoided church out of some misplaced sense of loyalty to her father, had only hurt her and pushed her further away from the very things that were dear and meaningful to her.

The service came to an end with the usual heartfelt prayers and Sunday announcements. Everyone was invited to stay for coffee and cookies in the fellowship hall, so the crowd began the laughing, cheerful migration in that direction. Carlie finally gathered up enough courage to glance at TJ.

"Are you up for some coffee in a crowd?" he asked.

"I thought we were supposed to meet Mrs. Brown in the church office."

"We are, but I guarantee it'll take her just as long to get through the cookie line as it will us. Come on."

He led the way, greeting people as they went. He seemed as warm and friendly today as he had been cool and dismissive on Thursday. What had happened in Louisville to bring such a change in his demeanor? She was almost afraid to ask.

Her mother caught up with them in the fellowship hall, just as they reached the coffee station. Mom greeted her with the same beaming smile that she'd been giving everyone. Carlie smiled back. Whatever their relationship was, she'd make the best of it.

"The choir sounded great, Mom."

"Thank you! I'm so glad you could be here, Carlie. And it's nice to see you again, Detective Douglas."

"How are you this morning, Mrs. Fenton? Can I get you a coffee?" TJ asked as he filled a cup.

"No, thank you. Bob and I are going out to brunch. We're meeting up with friends. Want to come?"

"We can't. We're going over old church records today," Carlie reminded her.

"Oh, that's right."

Bob arrived at her side. Carlie was polite and introduced him to TJ, but Bob and Mom were in a hurry, so the awkward conversation didn't have to continue.

TJ handed Carlie a cup of coffee. "Your mom's beau?"

"Yeah. I'm still not used to it."

"It's weird when our parents date."

"Absolutely. Does your mom have a significant other?"

"I think she's been seeing someone recently, but I'm usually happier if I don't know about it. When she gets serious, then she tells me."

"Did you have a stepdad?"

"No, she never let anyone get that serious. She always said her boys came first. Not a lot of men want to come in third place."

Carlie could understand that and respected TJ's mother even more. They threaded their way through various groups of people, all chatting and mingling. Kids darted about, giggling and earning harsh looks from their parents. It was just an ordinary day in church. Why had Carlie never felt at home here?

"Hey, this way," TJ said.

He took a quick detour past the welcome desk and pushed open an unmarked door. They were in a long hallway that Carlie had never encountered before.

"Where are we?" she asked.

"A sneaky, back way into the offices," he said, guiding her along. "Instead of going around the front of the building, we can cut through here. It's not fancy, though. The janitor's room is over there, the furnace room is there, and that door leads out by the dumpster. But this door takes us directly to the main reception area."

He pushed through another door, and sure enough, they had come to the other side of the building where the offices and preschool department were. Carlie was impressed.

"You obviously spend a lot more time in church than I do these days."

"Don't make too much of it." He laughed. "I mainly know my way around, because sometimes, I stop in when Matt's working here with his kids. They're PKs, so they spend a lot of time here. I stop in. We play hide-and-seek. It lets Matt and Wendy get stuff done, and I get to hang out with my nieces and nephew."

"They're really adorable."

"It runs in the family," he said.

"Careful, pride comes before a fall."

"I'll watch my step. It looks like we're the first ones here, though."

"I saw Bev back in the fellowship hall. Are you sure she remembers to meet us?"

"I talked to her when I got here today. She assured me she hasn't forgotten. I assume she'll be here in a minute or two. The filing room is locked up after hours, but we can just sit and wait. How's your coffee?"

"Just how I like it, thanks. But why don't we not talk about coffee and you can tell me what was so informative in Louisville. Did you track down any stolen property?"

"We did, actually, but not anything from our county. It looks like our thieves are selling the stuff elsewhere."

"I guess that's at least learning something. So what *did* you find out?"

"Well, mostly I learned what I already knew."

"Which is?"

"That I was kind of a jerk before I left, and I owe you an apology."

She nearly choked on her coffee. "I was not expecting that."

"Sorry. I was upset on Thursday, and I took it out on you. I shouldn't have, and I should have been honest and told you why I was rattled."

"What was going on? I know it was really rude of me to go through your possessions in the car, but I promise I didn't mean to."

"I know. I wasn't upset about that. It was just…a lot of things. I should probably tell you about Rissa, though, so you'll understand. We dated through high school, then into college. We were engaged, actually."

"Engaged! Wow. What happened?"

"Me. It was totally me. I was in college, working on getting ahead. You can relate, I think."

"Yeah."

"I'd grown up with Rissa—her family was in church with us. When we got engaged, everyone just expected a wedding right away. But I didn't want to start out with nothing. I wanted to wait. Every time she said we should set a date, I told her not yet."

"How long did she put up with that?"

"Three years. Then I went on to the academy. I told her to hang on just a little bit more. I guess she was tired of waiting by then. While I was gone, she met another man. Some rich guy—son of a local big shot—swept her off her feet. It was a whirlwind romance, and they were married before I got hired on at the police force."

"That's harsh. I'm so sorry."

"Don't feel sorry for me. I did enough of that myself—for too long. I stayed away from home, from church, from anybody who might be connected to her. Then she contacted me out of the blue one day, wanted to meet up, to try to be friends if we could. I didn't think I could."

"Did you try?"

"No. And that's all on me, too. I didn't even attempt it. She reached out to me a few times over the next years and I just blew her off."

"Well, she hurt you."

"No, she broke my heart, but she didn't hurt me. Her new husband was the one who liked hurting people. I didn't know it then, but he'd been abusing her almost from the start. She was reaching out to me for help, and I just pushed her away."

"But you didn't know!"

"If I hadn't stayed away, I would have. Somebody did. If I had stayed in contact with our friends, our church, I would have heard about it. I would've seen the signs. I could have done something."

"What happened to her?"

"She went to my mom. It was the middle of winter. She was black-and-blue, hadn't been allowed out of her house for days. She got away from him, and my mother took her in. She called me—that's when I finally got involved. I went over and took her to a shelter where he couldn't find her. She begged me not to tell anyone, not to bring police into it, and I gave in. For her sake, I agreed not to report. My mom gathered up clothes for her, and for a couple days, she was safe. We told her to talk to the pastor, to see what the church could do to help her."

"Did they help?"

"They helped her go back to him, that's what they did. That pastor said it was the right thing to do. I never talked to her again. Within a week, Rissa was dead."

Carlie felt her throat tighten. She resisted the urge to reach out to TJ, to touch him. His pain was evident as he related his story. She only wished there was something she could do.

"I'm so sorry, TJ. That's awful."

"I should have explained it on Thursday, why I was upset. It wasn't you, Carlie. It was just too many memories. If I could've told you, I would have. But Sheriff Villa ordered me not... Well, he'd just ordered me not to have anything to do with you during the investigation. I was trying to do the right thing by following orders, but all I did was make you think you'd done something wrong. I'm sorry for that."

"Why would the sheriff order you not to have anything to do with me? Oh, it's because he thinks my father might have killed Ricky, isn't it?"

"You're pretty smart…for a lawyer."

"Hey, what is it with you and lawyers anyway?" She knew he was joking this time, but he had—more than once—hinted that lawyers weren't his favorite people.

"Oh. I guess I owe you an apology and an explanation for that, too. The law firm that represented Rissa's husband? You guessed it—Blakely & Burke."

"Wait, was that the case with the son of the big real estate developer? That was her husband?"

"That's the one. His family had all the money they needed to mount a fabulous defense. Since Rissa had never reported any of the abuse—out of fear, out of shame or whatever—there wasn't a lot of evidence."

"You said she was pretty banged up."

"When she died, all her injuries were fresh—the old ones had apparently healed. Her husband said she fell down the stairs. There was enough alcohol in her system to make a convincing argument that she was a sloppy drunk who couldn't walk straight. It was his word against her family's, and they didn't have fancy lawyers."

"How awful. No wonder you aren't a big fan of lawyers. This sort of thing happens too often, I'm afraid. Your friend's case wasn't the only one I saw that made me wonder how my coworkers could sleep at night."

"Is that why you left?"

"I realized that I couldn't find what I wanted there. I wanted to help someone, to make a difference. I thought maybe I'd have a better chance of that here."

"And you will!"

She shook her head. "Not the way I hoped to. The bank turned down my loan. Between that and the newspaper articles, my father won't have much legacy left. I'm not being any help to him or his memory at all."

"Are you kidding? No man could possibly want a better legacy than what he left behind. He must've been so proud of you, the kind of person you are and what you've accomplished. As for his church, he didn't leave behind a building, he left behind people who truly care about each other, who carry on his work sharing the Gospel and reaching others. I know I certainly felt loved when I started coming to this church. Yes, Faith and Epiphany are combined now, but hasn't that just made your father's legacy twice as powerful? He touched so many lives, and now they are touching so many others."

"I have to admit, I never thought about it that way, TJ."

"Well, you should. It doesn't matter if you fix up that old building or not. You want to fix people's lives, and that's what you're doing. Just look, you already got me to trust an attorney!"

She laughed. He was teasing, of course, but she appreciated it. She was glad that he trusted her. Even better, she trusted him, too. No matter what happened from here, she knew she could count on TJ to give her father a chance. He would do all that he could to find the real murderer and bring justice for Ricky and for her father.

"Thanks, TJ. You're not too bad."

"Not too bad for a cop?"

"Not too bad for anyone."

Chapter Sixteen

TJ tried not to read too much into Carlie's compliment. He'd been hesitant to even tell her the whole story of his past failure with Rissa, but after his behavior toward her, she deserved the truth. He'd come to enjoy working with her, and the sheriff's unexpected order to stop had upset him more than he'd wanted to admit. It was too much, at the time, to abandon Carlie and dig into his memories of Rissa and all the opportunities he'd missed there.

He was going to try not to miss any with Carlie. He'd just have to be careful not to cross any ethical boundaries or go against any procedures along the way. He'd already decided that Carlie's presence here today, to go through the church records, was purely as a valuable witness.

One who made him laugh as she slurped down the rest of her coffee.

"Sorry, it's really good and I didn't have time for any before I left home this morning," she said sheepishly.

Fortunately, she was spared the teasing remark he

was already formulating when Mrs. Brown came bustling in through the main hallway. She held a plate of cookies in one hand and jangled a hefty key ring in the other.

She made flustered apologies for "gabbing" too long in the fellowship hall and greeted Carlie warmly. How long had it been since they'd seen each other? Carlie couldn't remember but said it was good to see her again.

TJ was impressed with her graciousness. Clearly, being here, being with people from her past brought back bittersweet memories for her, but Carlie didn't let any of that show. She'd shared only warmth with everyone he'd seen her interact with today.

Mrs. Brown unlocked the door and flipped on the lights in the filing room. A long conference table filled the center of the area, along with several chairs. Bev deposited her things on the table and went to a pair of old, somewhat-battered filing cabinets in the back corner.

"These are from Epiphany," she said. "Little by little, some of us old fogies have been working to scan all the documentation so we have digital records, but for now, the best chance for finding something is to search the physical files."

"It's great that you've kept them all this time," Carlie said.

TJ agreed.

Mrs. Brown beamed, obviously proud of her work for the church. "Of course! There are wedding records and baptismal records going all the way back to when the church was founded in 1874. That's fifteen years older than Faith Community. Did you know Faith was started by a group from Epiphany who wanted to build a mission congregation for people in town? Back then, it wasn't so easy to drive all that way with just horses and buggies. So really, Epiphany and Faith have been connected since the start. Besides, we're all one body, aren't we?"

"That we are," TJ said.

They decided to start looking at files from the months leading up to the excavation of the foundation. There were notes and minutes from board meetings and voter assemblies, tracking the evolution of the project. By autumn of the year before Ricky's disappearance, three quotes from excavation companies were submitted to the congregation for approval.

"So which company did they end up working with?" Carlie asked, shuffling papers in her search for the answer.

"Oh, that's simple," Bev said. "They went with my son's company, Brown & McCall Excavating."

Carlie brightened, then looked confused. "I had totally forgotten about that. But… McCall?"

"Yeah, Bob McCall. He was my son Bart's business partner."

"My mom's friend Bob? I thought he was into real estate."

"Oh sure, he's been doing that for a while now," Bev explained. "Twelve years ago, though, he was in excavating. He let Bart buy him out about nine, ten years ago when Bob's wife got sick with the cancer, poor thing. He cared for her for two years. After she passed, he went into real estate."

"I didn't realize that." Carlie seemed both surprised and unsettled by the information.

TJ had detected her coolness toward Bob, but she'd not said anything that indicated she had any real suspicions about him. Did she now think that her mom's boyfriend had been somehow involved in what happened to Ricky?

"We've now got the paper trail leading up to the start of the project," TJ said. "What was going on when the project ended?"

That, of course, was at the heart of the matter. Everyone seemed to recall that the project had stopped abruptly, but no one remembered why. These files might answer that question.

Carlie pulled up a small stack of papers stapled together.

"Here's a report from Bob McCall. It looks like their findings on the damage discovered at the foundation. It says they applied some kind of coating, but here's a quote for additional work in the future. It's dated in April."

"Did they end up doing that work?" TJ asked.

"I don't know," Carlie said, leafing through more papers.

"Well, here's a letter from the church," Bev said as they all scanned the files spread over the table. "It seems to be a request for work to stop."

That sounded like what they were looking for. TJ examined it carefully. As Mrs. Brown said, it was indeed a stop-work order from the church. Printed on official church letterhead, it thanked the Brown & McCall workers for their efforts. He read it aloud for Carlie's benefit.

"'For now, we think the work is enough to get by.

The church decided that we should wait before doing any other work on the foundation, so we'd like to have the hole filled in as soon as possible. Please do not disturb the area and risk damaging the work already done. Sincerely, Reverend Fenton.'"

Carlie listened carefully, then sighed. "So my father is the one who stopped the work."

"I guess so," TJ said, but continued to study the letter. "He's the one who signed this, but did he do his own typing?"

"He usually did," Carlie replied. "He liked writing, so he never minded typing his own letters. He said the church secretary was busy enough with newsletters and bulletins and things."

"How was his spelling?" TJ asked.

"He was a perfectionist. Why?"

TJ pushed the letter toward her and she frowned as she read.

"This does not look like something my father would send. Look at all the typos, and he misspelled *foundation*...and *damaging*. And this! This isn't even his signature!"

"Are you sure?"

"I know my own father's signature. He did *not* sign this letter, and I can't believe he typed it, either."

Bev Brown looked stunned. "It was with all the official papers in this file, and it's on the church letterhead. Who else would have done it?"

TJ met Carlie's eyes. "I don't know, but I'd sure like to know whose writing that is."

"I brought my yearbook," she said, instinctively understanding him. "I left it in my car...just in case."

* * *

Carlie helped gather up all the papers they had strewn over the table as TJ made a quick explanation to Mrs. Brown. He told her they might need to come back to gather some of these papers as evidence. He asked if he could get a quick photo of that stop-work order in the meantime. She said of course.

They left her to finish putting things away and rushed out to the parking lot. Carlie's car was sitting alone, so they made a beeline toward it. She was really glad she'd thought to bring the book.

Pulling it out, they laid the yearbook on the hood of her car. She opened it to the back pages where friends had written notes. She'd already studied them over the weekend so she knew what to look for.

"Here's something Ricky wrote," she said, pointing it out.

His writing was choppy, with long slashes through his *T*s. He hadn't been the one to sign the letter so she quickly moved on.

"This is the little poem Mitch wrote for me," she said.

TJ leaned in. Mitch's writing was much neater than Ricky's. It showed he put some care into it. The poem was about Carlie's smile being warm like a sunny day in a bright field of hay, but at least he'd put some thought into that, too.

"Does it match the signature at all?" she asked.

TJ held his phone next to the book. "It's hard to say. How does the signature compare to your father's? Do you think someone was trying to forge his name?"

"If they were, they didn't do a very good job. But yeah, maybe they did. They signed it with that big loop on the *R*, and he did sort of make the second bump on the *N* kind of flat."

"Then, maybe this is a match," TJ said. "The *E*s look the same, and the line over the *T* is the same. I'm not really an expert, though. What do you have for Scheuster's writing?"

"That's over here."

She flipped to another page. Dave Scheuster hadn't bothered with a poem, but he'd written a fun memory he had of hanging out with friends at Carlie's house and playing Ghost in the Graveyard after dark. Carlie wasn't sure she even recalled that event, but she was glad Scheuster had written about it.

"Does this match the signature?" she asked.

TJ studied it and compared to the image on his phone. "I don't think so. His letters are really round with big loops. It doesn't look at all the same to me."

Carlie sighed. It would have been so wonderful if they could have quickly found a match. As he said, though, maybe the person who signed the letter had disguised their writing and tried to make it look like her father's. They should have disguised their typos and misspellings a little better, though.

She suddenly had an idea.

"I don't suppose you have that postcard with you?" she asked.

He shook his head. "Sorry, I had to turn it in as evidence."

"Too bad. I would have liked to see how it compared."

But TJ was smiling at her and swiping at his phone.

"I didn't bring the postcard, but I did take a picture of it before I signed it in."

Sure enough, he held his phone out and expanded the photo. The text there was nice and clear. She held up the yearbook so they could both see.

"Um, I might be wrong, but does this postcard look an awful lot like the writing in your yearbook?" he said after a moment.

Carlie had just been thinking the same thing. "Yeah, it does. A lot like it."

She looked up at TJ and he looked at her. It was impossible not to smile.

"Scheuster sent the postcard," they both said in unison.

"Does that mean he's known all along Ricky is dead?" Carlie's mind reeled as all the implications of this became clear. "Has he been lying to Tamara all this time?"

They stared at each other. What on earth could Scheuster have gained by keeping his wife's hope alive that way? It made no sense—she just couldn't wrap her head around it.

"Do you think he sent all three of the postcards or just this one?" she asked.

"His wife seemed to think the same person sent all of them," TJ said.

"But wouldn't she have known her own husband's handwriting?"

She read the look on TJ's face and knew what he was going to say before he said it.

"Maybe she did."

Carlie gasped out loud. "And that's why she destroyed them and didn't tell anyone about them!"

"If this one hadn't already been misplaced somewhere, she probably would have trashed it, too," he pointed out, "once she realized it was Scheuster's handwriting."

"Poor Tamara! Maybe she didn't see it at first. After they were married awhile, though… I wonder how long it took before she acknowledged the truth."

"Obviously, this changes everything."

Carlie was still trying to mentally put all the pieces together. "Does this mean he murdered Ricky?"

"It means my job just got a little harder. Investigating a fellow officer is never a fun task."

"Worse than investigating a minister?"

"Almost as bad—especially if the minister has an overly persistent daughter who just won't stop poking her nose into the investigation."

"Have I really been such a pain?"

"No, you've been a big help, actually. All we need now is—"

He was interrupted by the sound of laughter coming from the church entrance. Mrs. Brown came rushing out, her phone to her ear and her voice loud and excited. She waved when she saw them and called over to share some good news.

"It was good seeing you two, but I've got to run! I just got a text. My grandson is back in town and I haven't seen him in ages!"

Carlie smiled and waved back, happy the woman was obviously so thrilled. Then Carlie put a couple more of the puzzle pieces together.

"Do you mean Mitch?" she called to Mrs. Brown. "Mitch has come back?"

The woman nodded, beaming. "Yes, isn't it wonderful? He's over at my son Bart's house right now."

She went back to her phone, laughing and obviously sharing the good news with someone else. Carlie turned to TJ to explain, just in case he hadn't caught on.

"Her grandson is Mitchell Brown," she said. "The third musketeer."

"And do you happen to know where her son Bart lives?"

Carlie grinned and nodded. "I do. Sometimes, it's good to be from a small town."

Chapter Seventeen

TJ drove along the country roads, letting Carlie direct him. She didn't know the actual address of Bart Brown's farm, but she knew what road to tell him to turn on. TJ supposed he could have forced her to stay behind, and he could've had Dispatch find the address for him, but this was much quicker.

Besides, he enjoyed spending time with Carlie. He'd realized that while he was away. He'd visited his mother and she'd pried and pried about his daily life in his new job. He'd made the mistake of mentioning Carlie. More than once. His mom had picked up on it, of course. She'd pried some more, and TJ realized he had quite a lot to say about Carlie, in fact. His mother had hung on every word.

First, he'd told her how Carlie was stubborn and overly demanding. He'd told her how Carlie refused to trust him to do his job properly. Then he'd told her of Carlie's unwavering confidence in her father, her lifelong faith and devotion to the church and her dreams of establishing an office that would not only provide legal help for people but social resources, as well. Finally he'd told her how Carlie's eyes always lit up when she smiled and how she'd laughed when he'd dumped spaghetti all over her.

It was about that time he'd realized he'd been gone only two days and already missed her. His mother had had the good sense just to laugh at him but not say anything. She didn't need to. TJ had been talking enough for both of them.

"Turn here onto Encampment Road," Carlie said.

He readily complied.

"There it is, on the right," she said, pointing to a rustic drive lined by trees.

The name Brown was on the mailbox, so TJ pulled in. The house sat up on a hill and the driveway wound toward it. As they neared, it seemed the Brown family was hosting a party. Five or six cars filled the gravel area beside the house.

"Hey, that's my mom's car!" Carlie said.

TJ pulled to a stop. Several people could be seen just around the corner of the garage. Carlie hopped out and TJ followed.

Sure enough, Carlie's mother was there. Her friend Bob was with her. Another couple about their age stood with them on a patio, chatting. Mrs. Brown had arrived too and was with the group.

"Carlie! What are you doing here?" her mother asked as they approached.

"I was just going to ask you the same thing, Mom," Carlie said.

"We came by to meet Bart and Amanda for lunch," Mrs. Fenton said. "I told you we had plans today."

"You did." Carlie nodded. "I just didn't expect it to be *here*."

The elder Mrs. Brown was delighted to see Carlie and TJ again so soon after leaving them at the church. She quickly made introductions.

"Bart, you remember Carlie Fenton. And this is Detective Douglas."

Bart stepped forward to greet them and introduced the woman next to him as his wife, Amanda. She was as friendly as her husband and insisted the newcomers join them on the back patio for some iced tea. The wonderful smell of meat cooking on a grill made TJ's mouth water. He would have rather stayed away from the grill and had less small talk, but sometimes, it was best to be a little more casual and avoid creating unnecessary tension. He smiled and cordially accepted Mrs. Brown's invitation.

"I'm sorry to interrupt your lunch," TJ said as they all moved onto the patio.

Bart laughed. "Oh, the more, the merrier! We've got a crowd, as you can see. Our son Mitch decided to turn up out of the blue."

A quick glance determined that although Mitch might be at his parents' house, he was not out here on the patio.

"Mrs. Brown mentioned back at the church that he'd come home," Carlie said with one of her brightest smiles. "How wonderful. I heard he'd been gone for a while."

"Yeah, he tends to go off and forget to let us know where he is," Bart said with just a hint of frustration. "Last time we heard from him was Christmas. Then he called to check in yesterday. Now today, he shows up! It's a nice surprise."

"I can imagine," TJ said. "Is he around? Do you think we could—"

This time, the interruption came from the rapid churning of gravel and the sound of a car practically roaring up the driveway. TJ peered around the garage to see another sheriff's cruiser lurch to a stop. Dave Scheuster jumped from it and came stalking their way.

"Where's my wife?" he demanded. "Her car's here. Where is Tamara?"

TJ was immediately on his guard. Everything about Scheuster's demeanor seemed keyed up and ready for a fight. He stepped in quickly to intercept his coworker.

"Hey, Scheuster. I just got here, but I haven't seen your wife."

"Her car's here," Scheuster repeated. "She's with Mitch, isn't she?"

Mr. Brown clearly sensed Scheuster's agitation, as well. He stood at TJ's shoulder.

"She's here, yes," the older man said. "She got here a few minutes ago. She's inside with Mitchell."

"Well, I need to see her. Him, too!"

Scheuster was just short of bellowing. TJ did not like where this was going. With everything he and Carlie had discovered, Scheuster's anger and Mitch's sudden appearance could spell trouble. It was going to be in everyone's best interest if he could keep the two men apart for now.

"What do you need, Scheuster?" TJ asked. "Whatever it is, we can talk through it if you'll just calm down. You're in uniform, and this is not the place to—"

"Dave!"

Everyone turned to see Tamara come rushing out the back door onto the patio. TJ could feel himself losing control of the situation. He positioned himself in front of his detective, but Scheuster dodged to get around him.

Just as Scheuster pushed TJ aside and practically tossed a chair out of his way to get across the concrete, a young man appeared in the doorway behind Tamara. Scheuster froze in his tracks. The man stepped out onto the stoop; this had to be Mitch.

The two men locked eyes, and the air practically sizzled with animosity.

Scheuster growled at his wife. "What has this guy been telling you?"

She was nervous, and her gaze flicked from person to person. Her words were purely for Scheuster, though.

"Nothing, babe. I just... I came by to say hi, that's all. We were talking about old times, stupid stuff, you know. He didn't tell me anything."

Scheuster moved to his wife, and she took hold of his arm, as if to prevent him from moving closer to Mitch. TJ glanced at Carlie. Her face had gone pale, and her eyes were wide. She blinked at him, seemingly shocked by the whole situation.

TJ knew that whatever was going on, it could escalate to something really bad, really fast. They weren't just dealing with estranged friends or marital discord here but twelve years of deception and murder. There was no telling what someone might do to keep certain secrets from coming out.

"Mitch, what's going on?" Mr. Brown asked.

"Nothing, Dad," Mitch replied evenly, his eyes never

leaving Scheuster. "My old buddy Dave just came by to pick up his wife."

"I just wonder how you convinced her to come over here in the first place," Scheuster said.

"Why don't you ask her?" Mitch said. "Looks like there's a nice big audience for whatever she might say."

"I'm not saying anything," Tamara said quickly. "Come on, Dave. Let's go."

Mitch just laughed at them both. "Yeah, you should go, Dave. Or maybe I'll start talking. Looks like there's plenty of people who would want to listen."

TJ could feel things coming to a boil. He needed to defuse the situation, but he also understood this might be his last chance to talk to Mitch. The man clearly knew something he felt might be damaging to someone, but he also had a proven tendency of disappearing. If TJ played this wrong, Mitch might just take off, carrying his information with him.

He supposed he could manipulate his way closer to Mitch and take him down, pinning him until he could get cuffs on. Could he trust Scheuster to back him up?

Whatever he needed to do, he wanted to be sure the others were safe. If it was time to act, he would have to become physical. Mitch would likely put up a fight and Scheuster might forget his training. At this point, the man was not acting like an officer of the law. TJ couldn't be sure any takedown attempt might not become violent. He needed the others to step back, out of harm's way. He looked to Carlie again. Would she understand his unspoken warning?

She nodded but didn't move. Instead, she smiled and reached to the cross hanging at her neck, just as she had earlier in church. In an instant, he knew what she meant. He was approaching this all wrong.

He didn't need to add to the tension—there was plenty of that. Introducing violence now was just asking for trouble. He needed to rely on something else. His brother's words from the sermon today ran through his soul: *What will you put on today?*

It was the right question for this moment. Would TJ put on anger and fear, or could he toss those aside? Would he approach this troubled man with judgment and violence, or would he choose patience and love? Would he put on charity now?

There truly was a time and a place for everything, and he felt very calm inside as he realized exactly what it was time for right now. He nodded back at Carlie and took one careful step toward Mitch. It was time for truth.

"We do want to listen, Mitch," TJ said. "Is there something you'd like to say?"

Mitch took a step back. He ran a shaking hand through his disheveled hair. His eyes darted anxiously. "I don't know you. Who are you?"

"I'm Detective Douglas. I've been investigating your friend's death."

"You don't know anything about that," Mitch grumbled. "Your coworker Scheuster might be able to tell you some things, though."

"Oh, I'll have a chat with Detective Scheuster. Don't worry about that," TJ said. "But right now, it seems like you might want to talk to me."

"None of you people want to hear what I have to say."

"Maybe not," TJ continued, taking another step forward, "but we need to hear it. I can understand you might want to protect someone, but you can't anymore. The truth is going to come out."

"No! It can't!"

TJ took a deep breath. His mind was racing, but he worked to keep his expression calm, his voice even and low. Mitch seemed to be a mess of anxiety and guilt. He felt such a wave of compassion for the man. His sunken eyes and sallow skin said it had been a long time since he'd taken care of himself. Whatever secrets he carried must have been eating at him all these years.

"Mitch, would it help if I told you what I know? Then you and Scheuster can just help me fill in the blanks."

Mitch shifted his gaze from TJ to his parents, then down to the ground. Behind him, TJ heard Tamara draw a worried breath and make something like a whimper. The grill sizzled quietly in the background, but no one moved.

"What have you found out?" Scheuster asked.

TJ could feel the conflict in the air around them begin to ease. Things were de-escalating. He knew he'd made the right choice.

"I found out that Ricky LeMaster died from blunt-force trauma to the head. He probably died instantly."

"That poor boy," the older Mrs. Brown said, shaking her head. "And none of us had any idea."

"Some of us had an idea," TJ corrected her. "And someone forged Reverend Fenton's name on the stop-work order so that the excavation site would be filled in ahead of schedule."

Bob McCall choked on the tea he'd just sipped. "I filled in that hole! I knew the job was coming to an end, so I didn't even question the stop-work order. You mean it wasn't legitimate? I actually buried that poor kid? Honestly, I never knew it."

"Ricky had been there more than a year when someone took on his identity and mailed a postcard to Tamara."

"Stop!" Tamara cried. "Don't say any more, please."

"The truth has to come out," TJ said gently. "Isn't it time everyone gives up the lies?"

"But maybe we can't ever really know what happened," Carlie's mom said. "Maybe some truth is just buried forever."

"Well, if you know that stop-work order was forged, who forged it?" Bart asked, eyeing his cowering son. "Do you know anything about that, Mitch?"

Mitch didn't answer, so TJ encouraged him. "I've compared some handwriting samples. We have a pretty good idea who it was."

Mitch finally looked up and met TJ's eyes. He took a deep breath. "Yeah. Okay, it was me. I found one of the letters the church had sent to your business, Dad, and I made a blank copy of the header. I typed up the stop-work order and printed it out. It looked like their real letterhead."

"You must have sent those postcards, too!" Scheuster shouted.

"No, Scheuster, he didn't," TJ said. "He probably didn't even know there was more than one postcard sent. But apparently you do."

Scheuster stammered and tried to say he hadn't meant to refer to more than one postcard, but his wife stopped him.

"Quiet, Dave. They know. I told them about all three postcards," she said, shaking her head sadly. "I just tried not to tell them they were from you."

"But I…" He gaped at TJ. "You *know*?"

"We checked the handwriting on that, too. I'm sorry, Scheuster, but you're in this up to your neck. We know the three of you were hanging out in the church parking lot that night. Something happened to Ricky and he never made it home. Why don't you do the right thing and tell the truth after all these years?"

Mitch's mom just couldn't stay quiet. She'd been wringing her hands as she listened and now seemed nearly in tears. "But Detective, they told the authorities all about that night twelve years ago when Ricky went missing. Go ahead, Mitch. Tell him… Tell it again. You boys were hanging out, trying to help Ricky get sober before you took him home. The minister came out and chased you away. You boys took Ricky home, then you never saw him again. Tell him!"

"He can't, Mrs. Brown. That's not really what happened," TJ said.

"Maybe they can't remember what happened," Carlie's mom interjected quickly. "It's been a long time."

"No, we remember," Scheuster said with a heavy sigh. "Every single day. Can't seem to forget."

His wife tried to silence him. "Dave, you don't have to say anything."

He looked at her with the saddest expression TJ had ever seen. "What does it matter now? You told them about the postcards. Did you know? Did you know all along they were from me?"

"No, not at first," she said earnestly. "I really believed… I wanted to believe. But then over time, when we never heard from Ricky again, I wondered. I realized that postcard I cherished wasn't in Ricky's handwriting but yours. Then when that next one came, I knew right away. You sent them whenever I was at a low point, when it seemed like maybe things weren't good between us. I told myself it was sweet, that it didn't mean you knew anything about Ricky, but that you cared about me. But I think I knew, deep down."

"That's why you never showed those other cards to anyone," Scheuster said, taking his wife's hands in his. "It drove me crazy, not knowing for sure if you got them!"

"I couldn't let anyone see them," she said. "Then they might think you knew something about Ricky. They might remember how you fought with him… how you gave him that black eye the day he went missing."

The emotion between the couple was intense. TJ kept a close eye on Mitch, just in case he thought about making a run for it. He didn't, though. He seemed as transfixed by the drama around him as everyone.

"I *did* know something about Ricky," Scheuster said quietly. "I never wanted you to find out, Tam, but I'm the one who killed him."

Tamara's brave expression crumbled as he spoke those words. Her eyes filled with tears as she clutched her husband's hands. "You, Dave? *You* killed him?"

"I'm so, so sorry," he mumbled, choking on the confession. "I promise I didn't mean to."

"How did it…? What happened?" Her tremulous voice broke.

"It was an accident. Yeah, Ricky and I had our differences, but he was my friend. I didn't mean to kill him. I was drunk that night—so much, I don't remember a lot. But we were driving around, spinning out in the gravel at the church parking lot. Being jerks. I guess Reverend Fenton came out and told us to go, but he went back inside. I don't remember what started it, but we got into an argument, and it ended up that Ricky wouldn't get in the car. I guess I got mad at him and was going to drive off and leave him. I was really out of it so I must have hit him with the car then passed out. Next thing I knew, Mitch was waking me up, saying we had to do something. We had to bury him and say he ran away. It was stupid and awful, but I just wasn't brave enough to do the right thing."

Everyone was silent. The story was tragic and painful. TJ would have given anything to go back in time and help those kids before they ruined everyone's lives. But there was no changing the past. At least now, with the truth being told, there was hope for the future. And forgiveness.

"But that's not what happened!" Carlie said suddenly. "That's still not the truth."

Chapter Eighteen

Carlie turned to her mother. "Why did you rip those pages out of Dad's journal?"

Her mom looked shocked. "I... What pages?"

"I know you did it. You were the only one who could have. I found them. I read them."

"But what...what did they say?"

Now it was Carlie's turn to be shocked. "You didn't read them?"

Her mom shook her head and looked completely embarrassed. "I didn't have time. I had just found the journal from that period, and I was going to read through it to make sure that... Well, I heard you and TJ arriving at the storage unit. So I just ripped those pages out."

"And hid them in the lamp," Carlie finished. "Yes, I found them there. But why, Mom? What did you think Dad had written in them?"

"What *did* he write?"

"He told about going out to the parking lot that night, seeing the guys there and worrying about them getting home safely. He knew two of them had been drinking.

So he told them to leave one of the cars there and the sober kid should drive the others home. He went back to bed, and in the morning, he was glad to see the cars were all gone and the gravel wasn't torn up too badly."

"That's all he wrote?"

"What else did you think he would say?"

"Well, he…" Her mom bit her lip, clearly unwilling to tell them any more. But what more could she have to tell? Did she know something about what happened to Ricky? Why would she worry that her father had written about it, whatever it was?

"If you know something, Mrs. Fenton, you really should tell us," TJ said. "The only way for any of this nightmare to be over is if we acknowledge the truth. All of it."

"I don't know anything else, not really," she said. "It was late at night. I woke up when my husband went out. I heard him come back inside and I heard a car drive away from the church. Whatever was going on was over, so I went back to sleep. Sometime later, though, I woke up again. Vance, my husband," she said, for TJ's benefit, "wasn't in bed. I heard noises again and I looked out the window. There were car lights at the church—two cars. I heard voices, too, but I couldn't hear what they were saying. There were more sounds of tires on gravel, then some yelling, and the car lights turned off. Then I saw something glinting over behind the church."

"You saw someone at the church?" Carlie asked.

"No, I couldn't see anyone, just some beams from a flashlight. It flicked around for a while, then it went off. After that, I heard the cars drive away, without their lights on. Your dad still wasn't around. So, I went out there to see if he was at the church. I could see where someone had been digging in the dirt, but no one was around, so I came back inside."

"And did you find Dad, then?"

"Yes, he was just coming out of the... He'd been washing his hands."

"So you thought he was the one who'd been digging in the dirt?"

"I didn't think anything at all at the time. He just said he'd been out to chase off some kids. We went back to bed, and it was a day or two before we heard that the LeMaster boy had gone missing."

"And then you started wondering if Dad knew more than he had told you."

"I don't know what I wondered. I just... He was a good man, but he wrote everything down. What if there was something he said, something he did that other people might not understand?"

"So you hid those pages, just in case." Carlie shook her head. "Mom, you didn't have to do that. Dad *was* a good man. He tried to help the boys that night. He'd been sleeping in the chair in the den. That's why you didn't see him."

"He put that in his journal? He was sleeping in the den?"

"Yes, and he didn't know anything about there being cars in the parking lot twice. Are you sure that's what you saw?"

"Honey, I've thought about it for years, trying to understand. That's exactly what I saw. I just never mentioned it because it didn't match the story your dad told or what the boys said."

"It didn't fit what your husband said, Mrs. Fenton, because he'd been asleep. He didn't know the boys came back a second time. And it didn't tally with what the boys disclosed because, well, they were trying to cover up Ricky's death."

"I don't remember going back a second time," Scheuster said, looking perplexed. "To be honest, I was really drunk. I don't remember much about that night."

"So why did you just tell us how you accidentally hit Ricky, then helped bury him?" TJ asked.

"Because Mitch told me what I did. I guess after I hit Ricky, I sobered up quick. I can remember the dirt… the awful, cold dirt on my friend…"

Tamara hung on her husband's arm, tears streaking her face. "You didn't mean to do it. You should have told me, Dave. You should have told all of us."

"I know. I'm so, so sorry."

"But I don't think you did it," Carlie insisted. "That's why you don't remember. You were unconscious. That's the one thing my dad wrote about that doesn't match your story. As I've always heard it, Ricky was too drunk to drive, so you guys were taking him home. But that's not what Dad wrote in his journal. He wrote that you were passed out in the car, Dave, and he was worried about you. He didn't want Mitch driving, either. He told Ricky to take you both home in his car. Obviously, someone came back again because his journal says that the next morning both vehicles were gone."

Now Mitch spoke up again. "Well, Scheuster wasn't unconscious! He remembers burying Ricky. Maybe… maybe I wasn't even there. Maybe that's who came back to the church, just Scheuster and Ricky."

"Carlie's mother saw two cars at that time, heard two cars drive away," TJ said.

"That's right," Scheuster said. "When I woke up, I was in the back seat of Ricky's car, and he was slumped over in the front seat. You were driving, Mitch, just driving around in the country. You told me what I did, that I tried to take off, but I hit Ricky, I passed out and now Ricky was dead. It was your idea to go back to the church and bury him in that work site."

Carlie studied Scheuster. His remorse felt honest and real. But something about the story still didn't quite fit. "If you were driving when Ricky was hit, how did you get in the back seat, Dave?"

He didn't seem to have an answer. Mitch jumped in to answer for him.

"I put him back there. I was worried. I thought we should get Ricky to the hospital. I put Scheuster in the back, Ricky in the front and was taking them both to the hospital."

Now Scheuster seemed to realize something didn't quite fit. "If we were going to the hospital, why were we out by the county line when I woke up? Yeah, Mitch, once you started telling me what you said I did, my head started to clear. I killed my best friend! I remember driving by the old quarry and thinking about how we used to sneak in there. That wasn't anywhere near the hospital, Mitch. Where were you really taking us?"

Mitch became defensive. "Look, all I did was try to help you guys, but it was too late for Ricky. Then I thought, at least I could help save your scholarship. Yeah, it was my idea to go back and bury Ricky, but only because I knew your life would be ruined if people found out what you did. I was trying to help you!"

"You should have taken us to the hospital or called someone, at least," Scheuster said. "You didn't help us, Mitch. You didn't help us at all. You ruined my life, convincing me to hide this and lie about everything."

"Oh, sure, your life is so ruined! You killed her brother, and Tamara still married you. You got to go to school, got to become the big, superhero cop. All of that because I never told anyone that you killed Ricky LeMaster! Ha, you know what's so funny? Your precious wife has known all along, and she still wants to stay with you! She's been paying me to keep quiet for several years now."

Scheuster stared at Tamara. "That's why you were over here? You've been paying him off?"

"He said if I didn't, he'd tell the sheriff."

Scheuster had some choice words for Mitch, and TJ had to step in to hold the detective from charging. Mitch's parents were in disbelief. The older Mrs. Brown fanned herself briskly.

"Yeah, okay. Sorry, Mom and Dad. I didn't come home to see you. I called yesterday, and when you mentioned you had lunch plans today, I figured you'd be out. I told Tamara to meet me here with another payment. I didn't count on a barbecue."

"You're a swine, Mitchell," Scheuster said. "Wasn't I already paying you enough?"

"You stopped paying me once Reverend Fenton died," Mitch practically snarled. "You said now that he was gone, there was no one who could dispute our version of the story—you could tell people I killed him just as easily as I could say you did. You blackmailed *me* into keeping quiet, just like I had done *you*."

"I never made you pay me," Scheuster said. "I lied about what happened because I thought... I thought it would cause less pain. Boy, was I wrong. All these years...so wrong."

"And I still think Mitch is lying," TJ said. "If Carlie's dad wrote that Scheuster was drunk in the back seat of the car, and that's where he remembers waking up a little while later, I'm wondering how he could have possibly been the one to drive the car that struck Ricky."

"You think I actually killed him?" Mitch said, trying to laugh. It sounded more like a frightened whimper.

"Yes, I do, Mitchell," TJ said. "Tell us the truth."

He still had that air of calm confidence, but there was a no-nonsense edge behind his words. Carlie watched his eyes, the cool intelligence there mixed with compassion and patience. Mitch was quiet, seemingly as transfixed by this man as Carlie was.

"All right," Mitch said finally. "Why not? Sure, you're right. It was me. All this time, it was me."

There were audible gasps. Scheuster seemed the most surprised of all. "It was *you*, Mitch?"

"You're such a sap, Scheuster! Yes, it was me. Reverend Fenton told Ricky to take us home. He knew I'd been drinking, just not as much as you had. But I knew if you got dropped off at home like you were, without your truck, your parents would go ballistic. They'd call my parents and we'd all get in trouble. So I told Ricky I was going to take the truck and follow him over to your place. He fought me on that, being all goody-goody, saying I shouldn't drive and that we gave our word to the reverend. Can you believe it? Our *word*? I tried to get into the truck and he pulled me out. I was mad, so I went and climbed in his car. I wasn't trying to hurt him! I just figured if I drove off in Ricky's, he'd have to follow along in the truck, and the keys were already in it. Then we'd be out of there, Fenton wouldn't call anyone, and nobody's parents would be any the wiser in the morning."

"But you struck Ricky with his car," TJ said.

Mitch nodded. "Yeah. I hit him hard. He was trying to stop me, to move in front so I couldn't drive. But he slipped on the gravel, I missed the brake and I hit him."

"Then you put him in the front seat and drove off," Carlie said. "My father could see your headlights from the house, but he had no idea what happened."

"I knew he was watching us," Mitch said. "And I panicked. I really did start off for the hospital, but it was too late. Ricky was gone. I didn't know what else to do! And then I remembered the work site. I remembered that my dad said he wasn't sure if the church was going to continue the job, and I remembered Scheuster was drunk in the back seat. I drove around until he woke up. Then I told him he'd killed Ricky and we went back to bury the body."

"So you guys left Ricky's car in another town?"

"Yeah. After we buried him, I took the car and Dave took the truck. We tried to be quiet. I didn't know you saw us then, Mrs. Fenton. We drove all the way to Friendsburg and left Ricky's car at a used car lot—figured it would be a few days before someone noticed it. Then we drove back here, and our parents just thought we had a late night. Which, I guess, was true."

"Thank you, Mitch," TJ said. "I'm sure that's been a heavy load to carry all these years."

"I sure didn't do myself any favors trying to hide it all this time," Mitch said. "I didn't do anything good for anyone."

It had been a very long day. The sun was setting, and TJ was finally able to leave the sheriff's office. His head hurt and his neck was sore from tension and sitting over his keyboard too long.

Scheuster and Mitch had been processed; Sheriff Villa had been briefed. He agreed that TJ had conducted an excellent investigation and was to be commended for such a swift resolution without any difficulties apprehending the suspects involved. No doubt the sheriff was drafting his next press release already, eager to brag about the efficiency of his team and to diffuse whatever backlash there might be that one of his deputies had just been charged in connection with the crime.

TJ had no idea what would happen to Detective Scheuster. He wouldn't be able to continue in his career and he'd have some difficult times ahead. Although he had not been the one to kill Ricky, he'd certainly obstructed justice. He would, no doubt, face multiple charges as the case worked its way through the courts. It did seem, however, that he had the love and support of his wife. That would help a lot, no matter how things went.

Mitch would face a tougher time. At this point, he was being charged with manslaughter. Other charges would follow due to his use of extortion and obstruction. He tried to seem hard and uncaring, but TJ could sense that he felt remorse. In time, he might come to find his way to repentance and be able to forgive himself.

TJ knew the real struggle now would be for everyone involved to come to terms with their grief and loss. Being deceived and carrying on a deception took its toll. All the lives that had been touched by Ricky's death and the circumstances around it would need time to heal.

He wondered how Carlie was handling things. She'd gone with her mother and Bob. Obviously, there were some issues that needed to be worked through there, and TJ hoped they could find their way to understanding. He wished he could be with her to help, but of course he could not. He'd been needed here, and Carlie's relationship with her mother was something only they could patch up.

Would he be interrupting or interfering if he called Carlie now? Surely, she'd want an update on the situation. If she was too busy with her mother or simply didn't want TJ around, she could tell him. If, however, she might like some company or support, he'd be happy to stop by.

Taking a chance, he sent her a quick text, in the guise of letting her know that everything had gone smoothly at his end and thanking her for her help. She texted back right away, thanking him for not giving up on her dad. She'd spent much of the afternoon with her mom, getting lunch with Bob and trying to know him better. Now she was meeting her mom at the cemetery to visit her father's grave. It seemed a fitting end to the day.

TJ was already in his car. He needed to pay his respects to the good reverend, too. For lots of reasons. He'd have just enough time to make a quick phone call on the way.

* * *

The sun was low. Long dappled shadows stretched over Carlie and her mother while golden rays filtered through the oak leaves. The cemetery at Epiphany Church was peaceful—it was as if all the intrigue and tragedy they'd been nearly swallowed by for so long had never happened. Her father's gravestone was serene, comforting. Carlie helped her mother lay a bouquet of bright flowers.

"He would be happy to see the truth finally known," her mother said.

"He would. And to know he had actually gotten through to Ricky. He'd been the sober one that night, and he'd tried to stop his friend from driving drunk. He tried to do what Dad asked and get his friends home."

"He wasn't a bad kid."

"None of them were." Carlie sighed. "They just made some really bad choices and tried to ignore the consequences. I hope they find some sort of peace after all this."

"I feel like I've made some bad choices too," her mom said.

Carlie looked at her, saw the pained worry in her eyes. She seemed tired, weary in a way Carlie had never seen.

"What do you mean, Mom?"

"I wasn't there for you after he died. I'm so sorry, Carlie. I tried to be strong, but I pushed you away and pushed everything else into a box."

"We were both struggling after he died so suddenly. You did what you could to try to keep me going. I might have quit school, come running back here and just given up. You didn't let me do that."

"I didn't let you grieve, though. I think it was because

I didn't want to let myself grieve. I'm sorry, Carlie. Suffering loss needs to be acknowledged. I should have let us feel it…together. That's another truth that shouldn't have been hidden."

"Well, it's out in the open now."

Even through the tears, her mother laughed. "I think something else is out in the open, too."

Carlie wasn't sure what she meant until she followed her mother's gaze. She hadn't heard a car arrive in the church parking lot on the other side of the building, so she was surprised to see someone walking toward them. The evening sunlight glowed around him as he approached.

"It looks like you and Detective Douglas make a pretty good team," her mother said quietly.

Carlie hushed her but couldn't hush the sudden increase in her heart rate. TJ was here, coming their way with a bouquet of his own.

"I thought I should come pay my respects, too," he said when he reached them at the gravesite. He stooped to add his flowers to the bunch they had placed. "Your husband must've been a really great guy, Mrs. Fenton."

"He was," she replied. "We only like really great guys in this family."

She gave Carlie a noticeable nudge with her elbow.

Carlie chuckled. "Okay, Mom. I promised I'd give Bob a chance."

Her mother gave Carlie another nudge. "I wasn't talking about Bob. Well, I'm going to head back home. I trust you can keep Carlie company for a while, Detective?"

"I'll certainly do my best, Mrs. Fenton."

Carlie winced in embarrassment at her mother's words, but all that did was get a chuckle from her as she turned to go.

With a parting grin, she said, "You'll do great, Detective."

Carlie waited for her to walk away before she felt composed enough to turn and meet TJ's gaze.

"What are you doing here?" she asked.

"I got all my work done and wanted to come pay my respects."

"You didn't even know my dad."

"But I know you. If you respect your dad, then I respect him, too. In fact, there's something I think you should see."

"What is it?"

He was pulling up an item on his phone. He held it out to show her.

"I was going through your father's day planners, trying to track Ricky's last days. I came across this."

She leaned in to get a better view. It appeared that he'd photographed an entry from a Saturday, two weeks before Ricky's disappearance. Her father had written "F + S group pm, trip to Lex."

She read that again, then suddenly it made sense. She caught her breath and she blinked up at TJ. He was a genius for discovering this entry and for obviously recognizing what it meant.

"I remember this!" she said. "The annual trip to the outreach center in Lexington. Our faith-and-service kids would take a trip somewhere every month to meet up with other youth groups for community service. We alternated—one month it was a morning trip, and the next month, it would be in the afternoon."

"As I searched through his planners, I found lots of entries like this," TJ said, smiling at her. "And do you notice how he writes it?"

"Yes. *F* and *S*, only he uses a little *T*-shaped symbol for the word *and*," Carlie said, smiling unabashedly back at him. "The entry that I found a few days ago didn't say anything about Fort Samuel! It was about the faith-and-service group meeting in the morning! He meant 'F + S a.m.,' *not* 'Ft Sam.' Whatever the trip was to be on that day, they must've canceled it. That's why he crossed it out."

"That's exactly what it was. I checked his journal entries and, sure enough, he wrote all about it. I know it wasn't easy for you to turn those day planners over to me, but thanks for trusting me."

"I didn't want to let you see that," she admitted. "But I knew my dad would want me to do the right thing."

"He seems like a truly good man. I'm glad I can get to know him through his journals."

She had to smile at the idea of TJ getting to know her father. Yes, they would have liked each other. "I wish you could have met him."

"Well, at least I know his legacy."

"You're right about that," she said. "I was wrong to think this old building was his legacy. It's not, and you helped me see that. He did leave a legacy behind, and no one can take that away, even if the building falls into the ground."

"But what if we can keep that from happening?"

"What do you mean?"

"I made a phone call. You know how I mentioned that I'd talked to the sheriff about needing some sort of program for young people?"

"Yes, and you said there weren't enough resources for that."

"Not within the sheriff's office, no. But I haven't stopped thinking about it. A couple weeks ago, my brother was telling me about how they'd love to expand the church facility to start opening up for more programs and youth events, but being in the middle of town, there isn't a lot of room for expansion."

"Wait, you think your brother's church could have use for Epiphany?"

"Not just the church. I liked what you were talking about, setting up your law offices along with social workers to help people in crisis. That certainly is a need we've seen from a law enforcement perspective, too."

"So what are you talking about?"

"Something more than a church, more than a youth center. A place that could meet the needs of whole families—access to counseling, legal services, job training, retreat facilities, emergency shelter, spiritual guidance, summer camp activities…all of it."

"Wow! That's quite a big project. I couldn't even get a loan to fix up the church for an office."

"No, you couldn't, because you're just one person. No one can do all this on their own, it's going to take all the churches, all the community groups, everyone who cares to work together. I talked to my brother, and he's already started a ministerial group who have been looking at some of these issues and considering possible solutions. When I mentioned that Epiphany could be used, and the parsonage, as well, he was very interested. He's going to talk to his group and the financers they've been conferring with. If I can get local law enforcement and other public agencies involved, we might just be able to make it happen."

"Do you really think so?"

"Yeah, I do. I mean, look at us. I told you to mind your own business and leave me alone. I figured I could solve that cold case on my own in a month. But you wouldn't give up! You made me work with you. Together, we solved this thing in a week. With a little more time together, Carlie, just think of what we can do."

She was almost afraid to ask. "Will we have more time for working together? I mean, now that you've got the case wrapped up and my father's name is secure, am I going to see you again?"

"I guess that's up to you."

"I suppose I could dig up a couple more forgotten homicides. That might get your attention."

"Oh, trust me, Carlie Fenton," TJ said, reaching out to pull her toward him. "You've had my attention right from the start. I was hoping you might come to feel the same way about me *without* another murder."

She smiled up at him, letting him hold her as she slipped her hands up to his shoulders. "Despite my best efforts, you've gotten under my skin, TJ Douglas. I can't seem to quit thinking about you…and I've tried."

"Yeah? I was already making excuses to spend time with you this week."

"What sort of excuses?"

"For one, there's that cleaning bill for your shirt that I ruined."

She shook her head. "Sorry, I presoaked it with some stuff my mom gave me. Worked wonders."

"All right, then. How about dinner? You never did get to finish your meal the other night. The least I could do is take you to Jack's Grill again."

"Okay, that's not bad. Any other excuses?"

"Well, there's my next investigation. I need you to help me determine whether our second kiss will be just as sweet as our first."

"But we haven't had a first kiss!"

He was grinning at her and holding her just a little bit tighter. "Then we should take care of that right now, shouldn't we?"

With the sunlight glittering around them and the birds offering a serenade, Carlie didn't even have to think twice. Her heart was full. Whatever was in store for them, she could trust TJ completely. She went on tiptoe to reach him.

"Absolutely."

Epilogue

The sanctuary at Epiphany Church gleamed under fresh paint and a year's worth of careful restorations. So much had happened! Carlie could hardly take it all in.

"Are you just about ready?" TJ said, walking up the long aisle to meet her. "The ceremony will be starting soon."

She knew people had already begun to gather outside. At precisely nine o'clock, she was supposed to meet them out there for a brief ceremony to officially cut the ribbon and invite everyone inside for Sunday morning worship. This would be the first service held here since the church had closed its doors after her father's death. She could practically feel him smiling down on them.

"Yeah, I think everything is in place," she said and checked her watch.

Unfortunately, she was also holding a cup of coffee in that hand. She caught it from spilling, but not before a few drops splashed onto the new dress she'd bought just for this occasion.

"Oh no!"

TJ just laughed at her and reached for a tissue from the box sitting at the end of the nearest pew. Carlie knew this would be an emotional day, so she'd insisted there be tissues for every row. She hadn't expected to put them to use due to her own clumsiness, though.

"It's okay," TJ said. "No one will notice. It's just a couple drops."

"I guess I'm a little bit nervous. I just want everything to go well."

"It will. You've worked really hard and it shows. Our partners and volunteers have done more than anyone thought possible in such a short time. Phase one of the Epiphany Project is going to be amazing."

She knew he was right; they'd had so much support from so many areas. Community groups, several churches and local governmental agencies had really come together to make this happen. The church building had been stabilized and refurbished to serve as a community center. It would provide meeting space for group sessions, seminars, continuing education and— of course—spiritual development.

The church offices and Sunday school rooms had been converted to office space for Carlie's legal practice and the first phase of their social service resources. As phase two kicked off later this summer, they would begin construction on the new community youth services and job-training facility. Remodeling on the parsonage was already underway to convert it to emergency housing for families and individuals in crisis.

She put her worries aside and smiled at TJ. He'd been at her side every step of the way over these past months.

Together, they'd prayed through the difficult days of the trials for Dave Scheuster and Mitch Brown. They'd consoled the families when both men were sentenced to pay for their respective crimes, and Carlie had dedicated some of the early efforts here to assist families of the incarcerated. When the two men finished serving their time, they would come home to families who were ready to love and support them.

TJ's insights and connections were invaluable. She'd come to lean on him in ways she never even knew she wanted to lean on someone. He'd charmed her mother and even let Bob teach him to golf. In turn, Carlie had helped convince his mother to finally move to Melfield.

In every way possible, they were ready to open the doors.

"All right," she said. "Let's do this."

"You've got your speech ready? Got the scissors for cutting the ribbon? You remembered to turn the lights on in the restrooms?" TJ asked.

"Yes, yes and yes," she replied with a laugh.

"Then, I guess you've thought of everything. Except…"

"What? What did I miss?"

"There's just one more thing. You picked out all the paint colors, organized the office layouts and selected the new carpet, but there's one more thing you need to decide on for Epiphany Chapel."

She felt a little panicked. "What is it?"

"Well, you need to decide if we're going to get married here, or at the big church in town."

To her absolute shock, TJ lowered himself onto one knee. He gazed up with those gorgeous green eyes and gave her a smile that would have melted her heart if it hadn't already been bursting from love.

"Will you marry me, Carlie? I'm hopelessly in love with you."

She almost didn't notice the ring he held up. She couldn't see it very well for the tears that came out of nowhere and filled her eyes. Apparently, she couldn't find words to speak, either. All she could do was nod frantically and find someplace to set her coffee cup so she could let TJ put the ring on her finger.

When he stood, she threw herself into his arms. It felt more like home than anywhere else she'd ever been. There was no doubt in her mind when she could finally verbalize her answer.

"Yes, TJ. I love you so much! Of course I'll marry you."

"But you didn't answer my first question," he said softly. "Do you want to get married here, in your father's church?"

She held him tighter and sighed.

"It doesn't matter if we get married here or somewhere else. It's just a building. What matters is the people who are with us, the people we love. The truth is, TJ, I'll marry you anywhere."

* * * * *

LOVE INSPIRED

Stories to uplift and inspire

Fall in love with Love Inspired—
inspirational and uplifting stories of faith
and hope. Find strength and comfort in
the bonds of friendship and community.
Revel in the warmth of possibility and the
promise of new beginnings.

Sign up for the Love Inspired newsletter
at **LoveInspired.com** to be the first
to find out about upcoming titles,
special promotions and exclusive content.

Get 4 FREE REWARDS!

We'll send you 2 FREE Books plus 2 FREE Mystery Gifts.

FREE
Value Over
$20

Both the **Love Inspired®** and **Love Inspired® Suspense** series feature compelling novels filled with inspirational romance, faith, forgiveness, and hope.

YES! Please send me 2 FREE novels from the Love Inspired or Love Inspired Suspense series and my 2 FREE gifts (gifts are worth about $10 retail). After receiving them, if I don't wish to receive any more books, I can return the shipping statement marked "cancel." If I don't cancel, I will receive 6 brand-new Love Inspired Larger-Print books or Love Inspired Suspense Larger-Print books every month and be billed just $5.99 each in the U.S. or $6.24 each in Canada. That is a savings of at least 17% off the cover price. It's quite a bargain! Shipping and handling is just 50¢ per book in the U.S. and $1.25 per book in Canada.* I understand that accepting the 2 free books and gifts places me under no obligation to buy anything. I can always return a shipment and cancel at any time. The free books and gifts are mine to keep no matter what I decide.

Choose one: ☐ **Love Inspired**
Larger-Print
(122/322 IDN GNWC)

☐ **Love Inspired Suspense**
Larger-Print
(107/307 IDN GNWN)

Name (please print)

Address   Apt. #

City   State/Province   Zip/Postal Code

Email: Please check this box ☐ if you would like to receive newsletters and promotional emails from Harlequin Enterprises ULC and its affiliates. You can unsubscribe anytime.

Mail to the Harlequin Reader Service:
IN U.S.A.: P.O. Box 1341, Buffalo, NY 14240-8531
IN CANADA: P.O. Box 603, Fort Erie, Ontario L2A 5X3

Want to try 2 free books from another series? Call 1-800-873-8635 or visit www.ReaderService.com.

*Terms and prices subject to change without notice. Prices do not include sales taxes, which will be charged (if applicable) based on your state or country of residence. Canadian residents will be charged applicable taxes. Offer not valid in Quebec. This offer is limited to one order per household. Books received may not be as shown. Not valid for current subscribers to the Love Inspired or Love Inspired Suspense series. All orders subject to approval. Credit or debit balances in a customer's account(s) may be offset by any other outstanding balance owed by or to the customer. Please allow 4 to 6 weeks for delivery. Offer available while quantities last.

Your Privacy—Your information is being collected by Harlequin Enterprises ULC, operating as Harlequin Reader Service. For a complete summary of the information we collect, how we use this information and to whom it is disclosed, please visit our privacy notice located at corporate.harlequin.com/privacy-notice. From time to time we may also exchange your personal information with reputable third parties. If you wish to opt out of this sharing of your personal information, please visit readerservice.com/consumerschoice or call 1-800-873-8635. **Notice to California Residents**—Under California law, you have specific rights to control and access your data. For more information on these rights and how to exercise them, visit corporate.harlequin.com/california-privacy.

LIRLIS22

In the darkness of her bedroom, Carina Collins jerked
awake, cold sweat coating her body. A scream welled
in her throat but remained trapped within her clenched
airway. The familiar nightmare always ended in that
noiseless scream, just as the memories of her abduction
when she was seven years old remained trapped in a deep,
dark compartment of her mind. The psychologists said
she might never recall what happened. As frustrating as
it was to live with a blank spot in her brain, she'd learned
to cope.

She lifted her head from her pillow and glanced
around the unfamiliar room. Moonbeams stole past the
edges of the window blinds and wrapped the space in
twilight, barely exposing geometric shapes of unopened
boxes squatting against the far wall. Where was she?
Oh, right. The move. She and her toddler son, Jace, had
relocated from Tulsa to small-town Argyle, Oklahoma,
only yesterday.

What had awakened her? Not the dream. A noise. Had Jace cried out?

Carina held her breath and listened. Silence from the direction of Jace's room. No, the sound seemed to float upward from the downstairs floorboards of the small 1950s-era home she'd leased. Surely she was imagining the stealthy tread. But the faint sound was too regular to be the random noises of a house settling. Then that first step at the bottom of the stairs let out its arthritic complaint.

Her pulse stuttered. It hadn't been her nightmare-stirred imagination. Someone was in the house and coming toward her.

Chills cascaded through Carina's body, threatening to paralyze her. She sucked in a breath and shook herself. She was twenty-seven now, not a child, and she had a baby to defend. Carina flung off her covers and sat up. Where was her cell phone? She needed to call for help. Her gut clenched. She'd left the cell downstairs on the charger. Why, oh why, hadn't she brought it up with her when she went to bed? Too late now.

God, please guide me to protect myself and Jace.

Don't miss
Unsolved Abduction *by Jill Elizabeth Nelson*
available wherever Love Inspired Suspense
books and ebooks are sold.

LoveInspired.com

LISEXP55500